The
Gosey

Dan Bomkamp

Lovstad Publishing
Poynette, Wisconsin
Lovstadpublishing@live.com

ISBN: 0692490337
ISBN-13: 978-0692490334
(Previous ISBN: 0615751555)

Printed in the United States of America

Cover design by Lovstad Publishing
Cover photo by Dan Bomkamp
On the cover: Cody Meckley, Alex Cole,
Tyler Cole & Ryan Salis

DEDICATION

This book is dedicated to Doug, Craig, and Duane; three of my boyhood friends with whom I shared many wonderful adventures. How lucky I was to have such friends as you!

Foreword

I grew up in a small village along the Wisconsin River. It is a sleepy place with friendly people who go to bed at night with their front doors unlocked and, often, with keys in the ignition of their cars. It is a place where everyone knows everyone and if anyone is in need, the whole village turns out to help.

Many people would think it would be boring to live in such a place. There were no malls, no movie theaters; no fast food. There wasn't even a traffic light. But if you were a kid who enjoyed poking around the marshes and the river, you never had a dull day. Our games centered on baseball, toy guns, fishing poles, and swimming. We didn't know what it was like to play video games or surf the Internet. The outdoors was our world.

It is a wonder that we attained adulthood. Without helmets, we miraculously survived many crashes on our one-speed bikes. We swam in the river without the advantage of a lifeguard and no one drowned-despite our mothers' warnings. Sleds with sharp metal edges or sheets of corrugated tin, serving as toboggans, carried us to the bottom of the sleighing hill. We used refrigerator boxes for make-believe tanks and crawled in them across streets and all over the neighborhood. We played war with toy guns and bows. Not one of us became a serial killer or a madman. So, I guess, in spite of the many politically incorrect games we played, we turned out okay.

I was lucky to have many good friends who shared childhood adventures with me. My three best friends are featured in this book. We have each gone our own way in life and, sadly, we don't see each other as often as we'd like. When we do, it's just like it was when we were kids. No matter how long it is between visits, we always have fun stuff to talk about and we end up reliving the adventures we shared when we were young.

Maybe we never totally grow up in our minds. No matter how old we become, that child still resides somewhere within. We can relive old memories and, for just a short while, be young, without a care in the world. Regardless of where we grow up, or what our interests are, each one of us has memories of unforgettable experiences and the great friends with whom we romped and played. Friendship is one of life's greatest gifts. I was so fortunate to have these fine friends as close companions. I hope they fondly recall the exploits chronicled in this book. And to the readers who grew up far from my little village of Muscoda, may the following adventures call you back to your childhood, rekindling comfortable memories of days gone by.

~~ Dan Bomkamp ~~

The Gosey

Prolog

St-Sauvin, Bordeaux region of France, Autumn 1839:

Henri Albert Gauthier was perched on the stone fence that surrounded his family garden. Beside him was his best friend, Philippe De Luc. The two boys were lifelong friends, born two days apart and living on farms that bordered each other. But this evening, Henri was daydreaming of a life far away. He watched the sun setting over the vineyards to the west of the family farm and thought of the life that he was planning in America.

"Are you sure you will go to America?" Philippe asked. "There is nothing to keep me here," Henri said. "America is a new land that has many opportunities. You should come, too."

"Henri! Come to supper," his mother called from the house. "I must go," he said to Philippe. "See you tomorrow." He jumped down from the stone wall and went to the house where his four brothers, three sisters, and parents were sitting around the large, wooden table, waiting for him.

Henri had finished school that spring and had been helping on the farm during the summer. Now he would harvest grapes and assist with wine making on neighboring farms. After the long winter, he would head to America. He had informed his parents of his dream and-while not overjoyed at his decision to leave home-they supported him and hoped he would find a good life in the New World. Henri and Philippe worked the grape-harvest duties together. Henri was not able to convince his friend to accompany him to America because Philippe was sweet on the neighbor's daughter and had his mind made up to make her his wife and settle down to a life of farming.

The following spring Henri boarded a ship in Calais, in Pasde-Calais, and soon he was sailing for his new life in America. He shared a stateroom with three other young French lads who were also looking for fame and wealth, and desiring to escape the farm and the poor conditions in their country. The ocean miles passed quickly and soon they were steaming into New York Harbor. Henri was amazed at the immense buildings and the throngs of scurrying people. The city was full of noise and smoke and aromas from food vendors. There were dozens of languages being spoken as people from all over the world lived in this wonderful, new place. He made his way through Immigration and soon found himself on a busy street in downtown New York City. One of his ship bunkmates who had a cousin living in Brooklyn invited Henri to accompany him to see this individual who could help them get a start in this new city.

The fellows located the cousin, who operated a bakery.

Cousin Charles was overjoyed to see the two young men and invited them to stay with his family until they could find jobs and lodging. Henri and Emile helped in the bakery each morning, getting up at 3 AM, and after the bread was baked, they went searching for work. Emile soon found employment at a butcher shop but Henri was not as lucky. In time he felt he was imposing on Charles and decided to look for his own place to live. But rent was too expensive.

One day a billboard caught his attention. A man named Col. William S. Hamilton of Wiota was searching for workers for lead mines and smelters in a place called Wisconsin. He offered "top dollar" to anyone answering his ad. The idea of going to a frontier town appealed to Henri who was tiring of the big city.

So he signed up, and a few days later, he boarded a train to Chicago. When he arrived at the train station, he was met by an employee of Col. Hamilton who put him on a buckboard wagon, along with a dozen other workers, and they headed north-to Wisconsin.

They arrived in an area called Mineral Point. They were given sleeping quarters and were taught how to work in the lead mines. It was hard, dirty work but the pay was good, the food was adequate, and when the men had time off, they delighted in the wonders of this new land. It was a beautiful part of the country with amazing wildlife, steep hills, and lush green valleys.

One day Col. Hamilton came to the mining camp recruiting workers for a new smelter in the north, in English Prairie. (Later English Prairie would be called Muscoda.) Henri and three of his fellow-miner friends volunteered to go, thinking that working at the smelter would be better than slaving in the dark, dirty mines.

They climbed on a wagon and, after a half day of traveling, found themselves in a small village along the Wisconsin River. The place was breathtaking! Tree-covered bluffs bordered the wide, clear river. Deer, squirrels, rabbits, ducks, and other game could be seen in abundance. The river was alive with fish of every kind. Col. Hamilton had built the smelter on the riverbank north of the village. They had constructed a large timber dock that flatboats could tie up to while they took on their loads of blocks of purified lead, called pigs. The flatboats were huge, thirty-feet wide and nearly seventy-feet long.

A small structure with open walls was built over the smelter to keep the rain out and behind was a bunkhouse for the workers. This place and the job were great improvements over Henri's former situation. He was happier than he had ever been.

In a few months he had saved a sum of money to send to his family in France. He included a letter telling them about this remarkable place, his work, and new friends. All in all, things could not have been better. The summer passed and the work carried on. Henri and his fellow workers reveled in their new environment.

Then the fall rains began and the weather turned cool. There was plenty of lead ore and Henri and his fellow workers labored on, thankful for the more moderate weather. Henri had made friends with the other three miners and they became like brothers. Two of them were from Cornwall, England, and one was from Bohemia. Their place of national origin did not matter, however, for now they were Americans. His fellow workers called Henri, Gosey, the Frenchman. Gauthier was pronounced Goay, but they thought Gosey was easier to pronounce. Henri didn't mind; in fact, he rather liked the nickname he had been given.

As the rains continued, the river began to rise and soon the gentle current in the river channel became a rushing torrent. The flatboats were now riding high in the water and instead of walking horizontally on the gangplank to load the boats, Henri and his workers had to walk uphill to access the boats. The gangplank was slick with rain and the turbulent channel caused the boat to rise and fall, making the job dangerous.

Henri had a canvas sling filled with lead pigs over his shoulders. Just as he got to the edge of the longboat, the current caused the boat to lurch, the gangplank jerked, and Henri tumbled into the water.

The sling was over his shoulders and the weighty lead pigs pulled him to the bottom of the river. He struggled and was able to free himself from the sling. He tried to swim to the surface, but the current pushed him under the flatboat. His head crashed into the bottom of the boat and he tried desperately to escape, but the current was so powerful that it pushed him farther under. He wasn't able to reach the bank side because the boat was tight against it.

Henri was panicking. He was desperate for air. His ears began to ring and he saw bright flashes of light in his eyes. He clawed the underside of the boat in a frantic attempt to break free. It was no use. The current was carrying him deeper. Finally he could hold his breath no longer. His lungs filled with water. He became calm and resigned himself to his fate. A picture of his mother, father, and family flashed in his mind. He felt no fear or pain; he just drifted off. Everything went black.

Henri's co-workers found his body two days later about a mile down river. Colonel Hamilton and Henri's friends gave him a funeral. They buried him on the riverbank near the site of the smelter. His friends planted a maple tree at his grave as a memorial. The tree had a large branch that pointed out over Henri's beloved river. As the years went by, the lead business underwent changes as more efficient smelters were built. Eventually the smelter on the banks of the Wisconsin River was abandoned. The smelter house and the bunkhouse burned down during a lightning storm. The rock foundations still sit on the riverbank and Henri's burial site has been preserved. The maple tree, with its branches stretching over the water, stands as a sentinel on the riverbank. To this day, the place is called the Gosey Hole.

School Daze

The summer I turned thirteen years old looked to be pretty much like all the other summers of my life, with one exception. I was finally going to be a teenager. No more little grade-school kid stuff for me. My friends and I were about to join the brotherhood of teenagers. But, first we had to finish seventh grade at St. John the Baptist Catholic School.

St. John the Baptist School; the kingdom of Sister Henry. She was principal, warden, and Reverend Mother of all the nuns, and she ruled like a czar. Sister Henry was a stern woman with a thin face that looked like it had never smiled. We called her "Hank" when she was safely out of earshot. She was the supreme ruler, the commander-in-chief, the sheriff, and she answered only to Father Lewandowski. Hank was the principal and taught seventh and eighth grades. When Hank was on patrol in the hallways, everyone was on best behavior. When school started in the morning, Hank stood at the end of the hall, watching. When the lunch bell rang, Hank stood at the end of the hall, watching. When school finished at the end of the day, Hank was right there again, watching for any misdeed, ready to grab the miscreant by the ear and haul him to the office. She was all-seeing, all-knowing, all-hearing.

Next in command was Sister Loratella. She was a heavy-set woman with a round face that was set in a permanent scowl. She was rumored to be a prison guard during World War II but we never found proof of this. There was no fooling around in Sister Loratella's classroom. If she caught you goofing off, she cracked you over the knuckles with her pointer. Now this was no ordinary pointer; not a little wisp of a stick used to point out words and numbers on the blackboard. No! This was a pointer made of many strips of wood laminated together in an intricate pattern with a diameter of about three- quarters of an inch. It looked like a work of art but it was really for cracking the knuckles of kids who whispered or made unacceptable noises in Sister Loratella's classroom. It was sturdy enough to use on the baseball diamond as a replacement for our bat if it ever came up missing. You didn't want to get a crack on the knuckles from Sister Loratella's pointer. Sister Loratella was fondly called, behind her back, Sister Tubatallow. Of course, no one, but no one, uttered her nickname loud enough to take a chance of getting a whack from the pointer.

Next in line was Sister Arsenia. She taught first, second, and third grades. Sister Arsenia, or Arsenic, as we called her, was a clone of Sister Loratella. In fact, there were those who said that they were cousins. Same shape, same face, same sunny disposition. The only thing missing was a pointer like her twin had. In its place was a heavy-duty yardstick, a complimentary gift from Krouskop's Lumber Yard on the occasion of their 20th anniversary. Arsenic was also the "lunch" sister. She rode herd over the kids in the lunch line and saw to it that no food was left on plates. If you tried to sneak carrots or broccoli into the wastebasket, she would whirl around like a radar antenna and stop you and insist that you eat the offending vegetable. "Just think of the starving children in China and how grateful they would be to have this food you're wasting," was her favorite saying. We often wanted to suggest that she get an envelope and we'd mail a few pounds of carrots to China, but, of course, we never were brave enough to recommend such a thing.

Then there was Sister Avonne. Why she became a nun, I'll never know. She was young, she was pretty, and she was nice.

She was our music teacher. Being twelve years old at the time, I thought she was the most beautiful woman in the world. Of course, I could only see her face and hands. The rest of her was covered by her habit, which made her look like a penguin with a Dixie cup on top of her head. But she was attractive. And she smiled, and laughed, and taught us to sing. Sister Avonne was my first crush; probably not the best choice of a girlfriend, but I was young and didn't know any better.

The lord and master of the school was Father Lewandowski. The nuns were "boss" when he wasn't around, but when he came to the school to visit or to see the nuns about parish business, they cowered in his presence. "Yes, Father! No, Father!" What Father wanted, Father got.

He was a nice man and we all were in awe of him, mostly because he struck such fear and obedience into the nuns. Anyone who could do that had to be powerful. Anyone who could make Tubatallow or Arsenic grovel was quite a guy in our eyes. Even Hank would wring her hands and follow him like a lost puppy when he was giving instructions about something he wanted done this way, or that way. And, he had a "hot" housekeeper.

The priests at St. John's always had a live-in housekeeper. They were usually old, rather frumpy ladies who cooked and cleaned for the priest and lived in the rectory with him. Father Lewandowski's housekeeper was Polly. She looked like Jayne Mansfield. Her dresses were bright red, tight, and sexy looking. She had blonde hair piled up high in a big hairdo. She smoked long cigarettes and held them in a holder that she carried like the wand of a fairy princess. She smelled like lilacs and roses and candy all mixed together. She was a babe! Of course, the boys at St. John's took every possible opportunity to check her out. There was never a shortage of volunteers when one of the nuns needed someone to run to the priest's house with a message for Father. Polly would answer the door and usually give the messenger a cookie or another treat. We could have

16

cared less about the cookie. We wanted to see Polly and be close to her. She "stood out" in our little town and turned the heads of much of the male populace.

Of course the wives of the town were very nice to Polly, but I'm sure they had a lot of things to say about her among themselves. If the women had their way, Polly would have been run out of town. But as long as she was Father's housekeeper, she was able to do as she pleased. It was fun to see Father and Polly attend a school play or music recital. Parishioners would sit on uncomfortable folding chairs in the school gym. Just before the curtain went up, Father and Polly would make their grand entrance and march down to the front and sit in plush, padded chairs that were put there especially for them. The only thing lacking was a trumpet fanfare-heralding the entrance of royalty, and flower girls scattering rose petals on the floor. It was good to be a priest. You were treated like a king.

We were nearing the end of the school year and my friends and I could hardly wait for summer vacation. There were fish to be caught; and there was swimming, baseball, and other adventures that we hadn't dreamed up yet. But first we had to endure that final week of school.

The days dragged on as if the whole world was in slow motion. The week seemed to last a year. The weather had warmed and it was torture sitting in a classroom. So, when Sister Henry asked for a volunteer to rake and clean up the playground in preparation for our school picnic, there was no shortage of offers. Anything was better than staying inside; even doing yard work.

Two of my best friends, Dewey and Chick, and I were assigned this task. That was good news for us because there was a chance that Polly would make an appearance and we were always glad to see her.

The three of us went over to Father's house which was on the corner of the school playground. We had two rakes and a galvanized washtub for hauling the leaves to the leaf pile on the other corner of the playground where they would be set afire and burned. Of course, first we had to bicker as to who would rake and who would haul the leaves. Not that it made a difference. We would end up taking turns but it seemed important to decide who was assigned what job.

Dewey wanted to rake. He didn't want to lug a washtub of leaves all the way across the playground. He liked jobs that took little effort and offered many breaks. Now, I'm not saying that Dewey was lazy, but he was definitely not overly ambitious. His world ran on a slower time clock than ours.

Dewey was of average height but he was on the "husky" side. He wasn't fat; just "chunky," as he always told us. "I'm big-boned," he said. Dewey never got excited, was never in a hurry, and was always hungry. He also had a little gas problem. "I have gastric distress in the lower tract," he would say just before he let one go. Of course, teenage boys thought that Dewey's talent was hilarious so he always received many laughs.

In all the years I had known Dewey, he had never once been on time for anything, except school; and he was late for that, too-about three times a week. No matter what it was-fishing, baseball, movies-Dewey was late. He even talked slowly. One time we had made plans to go fishing early on Saturday morning. Dewey's parents owned a steak house where they served food and beverages. They lived above the restaurant. I was up at dawn and had my fishing gear ready. I ate a quick breakfast and rode my bike to Dewey's. I climbed the stairs and knocked quietly on the door since I did not want to awaken his parents. No answer. I knocked again, a little louder, and I could hear someone walking in the apartment. Finally Dewey came to the door. He was in his underwear, scratching, and yawning.

"I thought you were gonna be ready!" I said.

Then, the standard answer from Dewey: "My alarm clock didn't go off."

Dewey had an alarm clock that managed to malfunction almost every day. I often suggested that he throw it in the river and buy a new one, but he insisted that it was just a little glitch and he thought he had it figured out. So, there I stood, in the living room of the apartment, waiting for Dewey.

"Hurry up! I'm ready to go," I said.

"I'll be ready in a couple of minutes," he mumbled as he waddled off scratching his behind.

I waited. I was dressed for fishing with my heavy jacket to keep off the morning chill. I also had my hip boots on, and I was getting hot standing in the warm apartment. Sweat began to form on my forehead, and I could feel a trickle running down the middle of my back. Suddenly, I could smell bacon! As much as I hated to walk into Dewey's apartment in my hip boots, I moved carefully toward the kitchen. There sat Dewey, still in his underwear, eating bacon and eggs, reading the morning newspaper. "What are you doing?" I asked, ready to blow a gasket.

He looked up at me like it was the most natural thing in the world and said, "Eating my breakfast! What does it look like?"

That was Dewey: never in a hurry, never on time, and always the last to arrive. You would have thought I'd be used to his habits.

Chick, on the other hand, was always on the go; rather like a shrew. Hurry up, and do this; then hurry up, and do that. Between Chick, moving at light speed, and Dewey, moving like a snail, I settled into the middle.

Chick was an import. He had moved to town a few years earlier from a big city. I met him at school the previous fall and we just sort of hit it off He didn't have a lot of friends at first but we quickly became good buddies. Coming from the city, it took him a while to get used to our small town. He was always full of ideas for things to do. And, most of them usually got us into trouble. Not that he was a bad influence; he just had ideas that frequently turned into disasters. He would come up with some hair-brained scheme and it usually didn't take much to get Dewey and me to go along with it.

We became friends because of something that we both loved: fishing. The first time I met him, he asked me if I fished. Fished? I lived to fish! I knew immediately I had a new friend. The following weekend, I took Chick to one of my favorite fishing spots in the river bottoms. It was a little river slough we called "The Little Cat." There was a spot where you could catch big bullheads and I showed it to him. You had to cast to an opening in the weeds about halfway across the slough. I cast to the spot and my bobber disappeared instantly and I reeled in a lunker bullhead. My next cast went to the same spot and I caught a second fish. Chick saw that the spot was vacant as I was taking the bullhead off and he reeled in his line to cast to my hotspot. He was in a big hurry and as I bent over to take my fish off, he swung his pole back and hooked me in the top of the head. I began yelling before he cast forward and tore my head off. His night crawler was hanging over my forehead between my eyes. Of course, he was regretful about hooking me, but he was also in a hurry to dislodge his hook so he could catch a fish. He had his priorities in the right place, according to my thinking.

Back to the clean-up job at the Father's house ... we went behind the house. We rounded the corner and there, sitting where we had left it about two months earlier, was what was left of the Giant Snowball. Actually, now it was a Giant Slushpile.

"Wow!" said Dewey, "Can you believe that?"

"No way! I thought it would be gone by now," Chick said. I just stood there with my mouth hanging open.

The Giant Snowball was one of those once-in-a-lifetime things. About two months earlier, we had a spring snowstorm that dumped nearly a foot of the most wonderful packing snow we had ever seen. School was called off for the day but Dewey and Chick and I had gone to the playground and built a snow fort. First, we went to the grocery store and asked Mr. Kalsher for several cardboard boxes that we took to the playground and filled with snow. We packed them tightly; then turned them over to create a rectangular slab of snow. We stacked these big white bricks until we had the best snow fort we had ever seen. Then, for an unknown reason, we started rolling a snowball. We went back and forth across the playground and the snowball grew bigger and bigger. Soon it was as tall as we were and, not long after, it far surpassed our height. We were barely able to move it. But, we didn't want to leave it behind, so we tried to roll it to my house two blocks away. We figured that if we left it on the playground, someone would steal it, and it was the biggest snowball we had ever seen; probably a world record. Well, we got to the back of Father's house and the Giant Snowball stopped, and we couldn't move it any farther. We tried to figure out what to do, finally deciding that the snowball would be safe in Father's yard, so we left it there. Who would steal a giant snowball from the yard of a priest? By the next day it no longer seemed important, so we just forgot about it. Now it was a pile of snow and slush, nothing like it had been.

"Well, we'll have to rake around it," I said. It was rather sad to see the Giant Snowball in such a pitiful state. It had been the biggest and best creation we had ever made, and we didn't know a snowball could last so long. We began raking and soon had enough leaves for Chick to haul to the burning pile. Dewey wanted to take a break while Chick transported the leaves but I kept raking. Next it was Dewey's turn to take the leaves and Chick took over on his rake. We worked around the yard, raking and hauling leaves, taking turns with the jobs. After an hour, we were finishing the job and it was my turn to haul. We had the washtub filled and I stepped inside and jumped up and down to mash the leaves so we could squeeze in a few more. At this time, Dewey decided that he needed to rest again. He dropped his rake and sat down in the grass. I squashed the leaves down as best I could and then I jumped out of the tub. My feet landed square on the up-pointed teeth of Dewey's rake. When my feet hit the rake teeth, the handle came up like a striking cobra and hit me between the eyes. I remember hearing a cracking sound, but nothing else.

The next thing I knew, I could smell this wonderful smell like lilacs and sweet candy. Then I could feel something cold on my forehead and soft hands stroking my hair. I struggled to get my eyes open and when I did, I thought I was in heaven and an angel was hovering over me.

"How do you feel?" the angel said.

"I'm good," I said. "Am I dead?"

The angel laughed. "No, you're not dead, but you have a nasty knot on your forehead. Does it hurt badly?"

"No, I'm good," I said. "Are you an angel?"

The angel laughed again and then I knew it was Polly! "No, not quite. Are you able to sit up?"

I tried to sit up, and Polly put her hands under my shoulders and helped me. She was kneeling next to me and began rubbing my back as I sat there.

"Just sit for a minute and get your bearings," she cooed.

I looked up and Dewey and Chick were standing there with their eyes about popping out of their heads. Polly put her arm around my shoulder and helped me up.

"There. Now how do you feel?" she asked. "I'm good."

"Do you want to come in and have a glass of milk?"

"Uh, yeah. That would be good." I was such a smooth conversationalist.

She took me inside, sat me at the kitchen table, poured a big glass of milk, and put several cookies on a plate for me.

"These will make you feel better. I've never seen a boy yet who didn't like cookies."

"Thank you, uh," I said. I had no idea what to call her. She wasn't "Mrs." and I didn't know her last name.

"Polly. Just call me, Polly," she said.

Polly. I could call her Polly! I took as long as I dared to eat the cookies and drink the milk. I wanted to make this last as long as possible. It was incredible watching Polly glide across the kitchen, working at her cooking chores. Finally I could stretch the cookies and milk no farther and, when I finished, I thanked

22

her and she walked me to the door. "You be careful, now," she said, and kissed me on top of the head. I almost fell down the steps!

Dewey and Chick were still standing in the yard with their mouths hanging open like a couple of bungling rattlebrains. When they saw her kissing my head, they almost had juvenile strokes. I walked down the steps and strutted over to my friends. "Boy, she makes good cookies," I said.

"Cookies? You got cookies?" Dewey asked.

"Yup, and a cold glass of milk, too. Polly's real nice."

"Polly? Nice?"

My status among the seventh grade boys at St. John the Baptist School had just risen to "super stud."

The School Picnic

Our school year culminated in a school picnic. It was a day of fun and games and lots of food. Instead of being inside and eating lunch in the cafeteria-which usually consisted of something very healthy, which we hated-we went outside, played games, and cooked hot dogs and marshmallows over an open fire. Not only did we like hot dogs and marshmallows much more than cafeteria food, we were also able to play with fire!

The sisters organized games for each age group. There were prizes and we had lots of fun. Of course, the older boys-like my buddies and me-weren't interested in those kiddy-games. Even if prizes were offered, we didn't participate. The prizes consisted of religious bookmarks or medals that had been blessed. If they had given packages of fishing hooks or baseball cards, we might have joined in. But, for holy stuff, we weren't interested and we went off to play either softball or "Bloody Murder." Now, as awful as the name sounds, "Bloody Murder" wasn't a terrible game about death and killing. A soccer ball was tossed on the playground. One boy, who was either extremely brave or stupid, would grab the ball and run with it. The rest of the players would chase him, screaming like wild savages, and when they caught him, they would pig-pile him. Eventually the ball would eject from the mass of screaming boys and someone would pick it up and take off running. That was our favorite game. It wasn't complicated. It involved running and shouting, dust and dirt, and the mayhem seemed to please everyone.

We played "Bloody Murder" for a couple of hours and then decided it was time to eat. We were covered in dust and sweat and there were generally a couple of bleeding elbows by that time, but nobody was injured enough to turn down hotdogs cooked over an open fire. Sister Arsenia was in charge of the food and she made us go to the school and wash up before cooking. Of course, that involved a lot of shouting and splashing water all over the restroom and, when we emerged, we were free of dust and dirt, but dripping wet. Then we each took a weenie stick-a branch from a lilac bush at Father's house that had been sharpened on one end-and inserted it into a weenie and held it over the fire. Not only was it great to be out of school and to be in the sunshine, but we also got to horse around with fire. There were about a dozen of us at the fire-pit cooking and eating hot dogs and potato chips and drinking Kool-Aid. There was no limit so, of course, we tried to surpass each other in the number of hot dogs consumed. Dewey was leading the pack with his eighth "dog" and there were no close contenders. Then Sister brought out a bag of marshmallows for roasting for dessert. There was only one thing that I liked more than roasted marshmallows, and that was s'mores: roasted marshmallows between two pieces of Hershey Bar and two graham crackers. Unfortunately, the nuns' budget didn't allow for Hershey Bars so we had to eat plain marshmallows.

I was roasting a marshmallow, and it was almost perfect. The trick was to hold it to the side of the flame so it became golden brown and gooey inside without turning black on the outside. If you didn't get it close enough to the fire, it stayed solid in the middle. If you got it too close, it turned black, and sometimes it caught on fire. It was a very delicate operation.

Anyway, my marshmallow was turning the most beautiful, golden-brown color, and Dewey was next to me, roasting one. He was always in a hurry to get it cooked so he could get another, so he held his directly in the fire. Of course, it burst into flames and turned black instantly. As he retrieved it, it touched my perfect specimen and ignited it. I quickly pulled my marshmallow out of the fire pit and blew on it attempting to salvage it.

Then I thought, rather than blow, I'd fan it, so as to not take the chance of burning myself I whipped my stick back and forth to extinguish the flames and, at that same second, David Kite ran past, chasing Chick, who had swiped his potato chips. The flaming marshmallow hit David behind his right ear and stuck to the side of his head! Of course, it was still on fire so it burned off a large patch of his hair.

When the flaming marshmallow hit him, David did exactly what we were taught not to do in safety class. He took off running, screaming like a banshee. Of course, everyone knows he should have stopped, dropped, and rolled. It happened quickly and I wasn't sure what had happened to my marshmallow. Then I saw David running across the playground with smoke coming from the side of his head. He was headed toward Sister Arsenia!

Dewey looked at me and said, "You're dead."

David got to Sister Arsenia. She grabbed him and put her denim apron, covering her habit, over his head to snuff out the fire. He was bawling and screaming. Somewhere, in all the confusion, I heard him mention my name and Sister glanced at me with a death-sentence look. I wanted to take off running for home I but knew she would get me in the end so I just reached for another marshmallow and tried to look innocent.

Sister Arsenia took David to the school and a few minutes later, Hank came out of the door, looking at me. I wanted to crawl under a rock; I even thought of running for the church and asking for sanctuary, but I couldn't move. I was so scared. Hank marched up to me and told me to follow her to the school.

It was the longest walk of my life. I had never been in Hank's office before. It was small with painted cement block walls. There was a bookcase and a file cabinet against the right wall and a picture of Pope Pius on the left wall. Behind the desk were two windows. And there sat David. His eyes were red; his nose was running, and he was blubbering. The hair on the right side of his head was gone and the office smelled like burnt chicken feathers. There was a big, red blister-about the size of a large marshmallow-behind his ear. Sister Arsenia had treated it with a gob of ointment that made David's head look greasy and nasty.

Sister Arsenia was standing behind David who was sitting in one of two wooden chairs in front of Hank's desk. Her apron was smeared with marshmallow and soot from David's burning head. Hank sat at her desk, put her hands together, and looked at me.

"Do you see what you did to poor David?" Hank asked.

"Yes, Sister."

"Do you feel badly for doing it?"

"Yes, Sister."

"What are you going to do about it?"

I didn't have the faintest idea of what she was asking. What did she expect me to do? Throw myself in front of a train; jump off a bridge? Maybe she wanted me to stick a flaming marshmallow on the side of my head. I had nothing to say, so I thought it would be best to rely on Hank's wisdom. "Um ... what do you think I should do, Sister?"

"You need to tell David that you're sorry and then go to the church and ask God's forgiveness."

Whew! That was easy. I didn't expect such a light sentence. I thought maybe my entire eighth-grade year would be spent in detention or I'd suffer another punishment; but an apology and a few "Hail Marys" weren't bad at all.

"David, I'm sorry. Please forgive me," I said, with all the earnestness I could muster. David blubbered something that must have been okay.

Hank motioned for me to follow her and we walked into the hallway. "You run over to the church and say a little prayer for David, and then go back to the picnic." And then she smiled at me. I had never seen Hank smile before! "I know you didn't do that on purpose, and I know you're a good boy, so let's just let it go at a little prayer, okay?"

"Yes, Sister Henry! Thank you." I ran as fast as I could to the church and said a little prayer for David, and then I threw in "thanks" for the good luck I had in the past few days with Polly, and now with Sister Henry. The summer was looking good.

Fishing

Ever since I was old enough to ride a two-wheel bike, I fished. Summer was for fishing and baseball. Nothing else was important, and fishing was my first love. Our house was about a mile from the Wisconsin River, but the river was off-limits. My mom insisted that I do my fishing in the sloughs where there weren't currents or whirlpools.

For some reason, my mother was an expert on currents and whirlpools. I doubt that she had ever even gotten her big toe wet in the river but she always warned me not to go there because a whirlpool would suck me under and drown me. I was required to fish in one of the river bottom sloughs where the water was shallow and the current was so slow that you could barely see it move.

There were many sloughs within bike-riding range so my friends and I had many places to fish. If it was a day when we only had a couple hours before a baseball game, we would go to the Cat. Actually there were two Cats; the Big Cat and the Little Cat. Both of the Cats were small sloughs and were close to town. We sat on the bank and fished mainly for bluegills and bullheads. Once in a while we caught a bass or a northern, or an ugly dogfish, but generally, just bluegills. We didn't care. As long as we were fishing, it didn't matter what we caught, how many, or how big. We were happy just to be fishing.

On the days we didn't play baseball, we went to Gutweiler's Lake. Now this was a real lake; not a little slough like the Cat. Gutweiler's was about three-quarters of a mile long and about a hundred yards across at its widest point. At the upper end, there was a small creek running into the lake, and at the lower end, the lake became a creek again. The creek meandered for a while through the woods and then emptied into the Wisconsin River. The water moved slowly from one slough to the next and eventually ended up back in the big river.

Gutweiler's was our favorite place to fish. There were lots of good-sized northern pike and bass, and the bluegills were much bigger than in the Cat. We could ride our bikes to the lower end and then cross the creek on a beaver dam if we wanted to fish on the marsh side of the lake. Otherwise we would fish on the high bank that bordered the woods. Often we would take our lunch and spend the whole day at the lake. If the fish weren't biting, we could look for frogs or wade around in the shallow water. Additionally, the woods had cool stuff for us to poke around in and we always found lots of interesting critters.

Standard attire for the summer was a short-sleeved cotton shirt, or a tee shirt-usually white-and cut-off blue jeans and tennis shoes. Even though our moms would buy us jeans each fall that were about four inches too long, we seemed to outgrow them fast enough to have a good supply of cut-offs for summer wear. Everyone had the same shoes. There was only one choice for tennis shoes. They were all high-top, black, and made of canvas. During the summer we wore them without socks, so after a few fishing trips-which included wading in the mud and a few innings of baseball in the hot sun-they became a bit aromatic. Of course, made of canvas, they were easy to wash, and most moms kept them from getting too rank.

While fishing, we generally took off our shirts so, after a while, we all looked like south-sea islanders. Everyone was the same. It was the standard uniform of the day. It made us all equal; all on the same team.

Not all my friends were from my class at St. John the Baptist School. In the summer, I also enjoyed the company of friends from the public school. Although the nuns would probably not have thought well of this, my friends and I associated freely with kids from the public school in the summertime. After all, if we were limited to only our friends from St. John's, there would not be enough players for a proper baseball game, so we had to include other kids, one of which became one of my best buddies.

His name was Dougie and he was an import kid. His family

had moved to our town the previous summer. His dad was a bigwig in the public school system. The family lived a short distance from my house and they had four boys. Dougie was my age and he had younger brothers the same age as my younger brothers, so my brothers and I got new friends.

One day that summer I was riding my bike down to the Cat for a couple of hours of fishing, and I rode past their house. Dougie was sitting on the front porch steps doing something with a fishing pole. Of course I noticed him immediately. Fishing poles always caught my attention. I had my pole and tackle box and a can of worms in my bike basket and, as I rode by, he looked up and waved at me. I wanted to get a better look at his fishing pole so I made a V-turn and pulled up in front of his house.

"Goin' fishin?" I asked.

"Naw. I don't know where the good spots are. I just moved here," he said.

I got off my bike and parked it and walked up to him. "Nice pole! Is it new?"

"Yeah. My grandma gave it to me for my birthday. Want to see it?"

Wow! Did I!! It was a spinning rod with a Mitchell 300 reel!

"Wow! This is cool. I've never used one of these reels," I said. I had always had the push-button reels and this was something new and wonderful-looking to me.

"Give it a throw," Dougie said.

He showed me how to open the bail and hold the line in my finger and then throw it. It cast like a dream, clear across the street.

"Whoa! This is really cool!" I said, reeling the line back up.

"You wanna go fishin' with me?"

"Sure."

He ran into the house and asked his mom if he could go. She came out and I told her about the Cat and how it was safe and she gave Dougie permission to go. She told us to wait a minute and soon she returned with a sack of homemade cookies. This was getting better all the time.

Well, Dougie and I went to the Cat. We fished, talked, and got to know each other and became friends, even if he was a public school kid.

From then on, Dewey, Chick, and Dougie were my constant companions. We fished, played baseball, swam, slept out, and spent the summer together. The four musketeers: one for all, and all for one.

One evening, when we were fishing at the Cat, the discussion turned to the book The Three Musketeers.

"I wonder why that Dumas guy didn't call it The Four Musketeers," Chick said.

"The first three guys were already Musketeers, and the D' Artagnan guy was a new recruit," I said.

"Kinda like Dougie; he's new in town and goes to the public school," Chick said.

"Yup! Just call me Dougie 'Tagnan," Dougie said. We all laughed at Dougie's joke.

A short time after our first experience fishing at the Cat, Dougie and I were fishing on the marsh side of Gutweiler's. Dewey and Chick had been required by their moms to do chores. Dougie and I decided it was not a good idea to hang around and take the chance that our moms would get wind of our friends doing home stuff, so we headed to the lake. The lower end of Gutweiler's narrowed before it reached the beaver dam where it became a stream that flowed into the river. Many trees had been blown down by summer storms and were lying in the water. We often caught fine fish around the downed trees, but on this day we were sitting, watching our bobbers, and there was no action. Dougie was always interested in poking around in the swamp, looking for creepy, slimy critters, and he had found a frog. He was attempting to get the frog to sit in the palm of his hand and soon he had the critter calmed down and it stayed put. Just as he began to brag about what a great frog-tamer he was, the frog

31

took a mighty leap and landed in the lake, about six feet from shore.

"Oh, yeah! The great frog-tamer," I laughed.

The frog decided it was a good idea to escape and just as he took a couple strokes, a huge large-mouth bass came up and gulped him off the surface.

"Wow! Look at that!" Dougie yelled. We both got the idea at the same time and took off running for the marsh. It didn't take us long to each capture a frog. We put them in our shorts pockets, reeled in our lines, removed our sinkers and bobbers and tied on our biggest hooks. Then we hooked the frogs through the lips and cast them into the lake, about ten feet apart. Neither frog had time to take a stroke because the water erupted and both of them were gulped down by two bass. We waited a couple of seconds and then set the hook. We both had a big bass on our lines at the same time. We fought the fish, back and forth, and finally landed them. We took them off quickly, put them on a stringer-which we tied to a tree branch-and then we ran off to look for more frogs. Dougie found one first and raced back to the lake. I could hear him yelling that he had another fish while I was still looking for a frog. I finally found one and caught it, and while I was racing for the lake, Dougie met me on his way back to go frog hunting again.

I don't know how long this procedure lasted, but finally we realized no more fish were biting. We waited and waited, and reeled in our frogs and cast them to another area, but the fish were gone; or we had caught them all.

"Wow!" Dougie panted. "I've never seen fishing like that in my whole life."

"Me, either," I said. We finally gave up and reeled in our frogs. They were both still in good shape so we carefully unhooked them and turned them loose. Then we lifted a stringer of six huge bass!

"I've never seen so many big fish on one stringer in my life," I said, admiring the fish.

"Me, either. Let's go show Dewey and Chick. They'll be so mad they had to stay home." Catching the fish was fun, but showing them off to our envious friends was almost better.

"Hey, let's take them to the newspaper office and see if they want a picture of this," Dougie said.

That sounded like a dandy idea to me, so we loaded up our gear and walked across the beaver dam to our bikes. Dougie had one basket on the front of his bike and I had double baskets on the back of mine, so we put all the fishing gear in my baskets and he took the fish. We rode our bikes as fast as we could to the local newspaper office-as if there were other groups of boys on their way at the same time and only one group would be featured in the paper. When we arrived, a newspaper reporter assessed our catch. He thought this would make a good story. He instructed us to lay them on the sidewalk and kneel behind them. He snapped our picture and asked us questions about our unbelievable success.

Of course his first question was, "Where did you catch them?"

I looked at Dougie and he was obviously trying to think of an answer that wouldn't give our hot-spot away.

"In the river bottoms," he said.

"I see. What did you use for bait?"

Again, our bait was something that we wanted to keep a secret, so I said, "Top-water baits."

"Top-water baits? Care to be more specific?"

"Nope."

He grinned and said that would be okay, and we took off for Dewey's and Chick's houses to show them what they had missed by working at home. Of course they were angry at us for catching fish without them, but if they had been there, it probably wouldn't have happened. Dewey would never have been quick enough to catch a frog and Chick would have been in such a hurry to get his frog into the water that he would have fallen in and scared the fish away.

We were on the front page of the newspaper the following

Thursday. We had a smug look on our faces and the accompanying story was that we were tight-lipped about the place and method of catching our fish but, suffice it to say, it must have been a secret weapon and we were probably the envy of the other fishermen in the area. We expected a contract from a fishing company to serve as spokesmen. Surely someone would want two expert fishermen to endorse their products, but sadly that didn't happen. We had to be satisfied with the glory of being two of the best and most famous fishermen among our gang of friends.

We never managed to get into the middle of a feeding frenzy like that again, but, for Dougie and me, it was an experience we would never forget.

Adventures in Chicago

During our seventh-grade year, we had endless bake sales, car washes, dances, lotteries, bingo nights, raffles, and candy sales to raise money for our class trip to Chicago. It had been in the planning for a year and now we were at the train station, standing in the morning darkness, waiting for the train to pick us up to take us to the big city.

There were kids and moms huddled in little groups on the train platform and in the depot. Every kid was receiving last minute instructions as to how to behave and orders to mind the sisters. Mom was making sure I had our phone number tucked safely into my shirt pocket and she was fussing over the way my hair was sticking up in the back. Just then we heard the sound of the approaching train and everyone began moving toward the platform. The boys were trying to put distance between them and their moms so they wouldn't have to suffer the indignity of a kiss in front of the other guys. Chick and Dewey were, likewise, getting their final instructions, but their moms might as well have been speaking Flemish to them as they weren't paying a bit of attention. They were struggling to get to the front of the line to board the train.

The lumbering locomotive came clanging into the station, great clouds of steam billowing out from the belly with a loud hissing sound as the engineer applied the brakes. The sisters were trying to get everyone in line so a head count could be taken and slowly, one by one, we were checked off the list on Sister Henry's clipboard. Dewey, Chick, and I passed by her, climbed on the train, and ran smack into Sister Arsenia. She was herding kids to seats and told us to go to the other end of the car, take a seat, and be quiet.

Soon everyone was on board and the train pulled away from the platform, heading for Chicago, so far away from our little town. Our moms waved and mouthed good- bye as we set off into the darkness. We were excited and chattering like a bunch of squirrels when a porter came through the car. He was a huge, black man, wearing a bright blue uniform with gold trim and a blue and gold cap that looked like a policeman's cap. He smiled at us as he passed and we smiled back, somewhat apprehensively. We had never seen a black man close up before and especially one that was so big. For most of us, the only black men we had ever seen were in the movies since there were none living in our town.

"Wow!" Dewey said. "I have never seen such a large, black man."

"You have never seen a black man before, period!" Chick said.

"Well, I guess you're right," Dewey said.

"He seemed nice," I said. We were all a bit in awe of the big man, not only because of his color, but because of his size. He was at least six and a half feet tall, had huge hands, and looked like a giant to a bunch of grade-school kids.

Soon the man returned to our car and said in a loud voice, "Ladies and gentlemen, your breakfast is served in the dining

Dewey looked at me. "Wow! This is great. We get food on the train, too." We took off, on the run, to be first to reach the dining car. There was a platform outside our car that butted up to a platform on the next car. The wind was howling between the cars and you could peer down and see track whizzing by. You had to step across the small gap between the two platforms to get to the next car. We crossed through three crowded cars in this manner before reaching the dining car. It was like a long narrow restaurant with booths on each side. Each booth had a table with a white tablecloth and a vase in the middle with a flower.

Dewey, Chick, another kid, Mike and I slid into a booth and a young, black man in a white waiter's jacket approached us and asked what we wanted to drink with breakfast. He was much younger than the other man and was about the size of most people we knew. He looked at us and held a little pad in his hand waiting for our drink orders.

"Whatcha got?" Dewey asked.

"We have milk, chocolate milk, orange juice, grapefruit juice, and soda," the man said.

"I'll have soda."

"Me, too," I said.

"Me, three," said Chick. We all burst out laughing at the joke, and the man in the white jacket laughed, too.

"And you, sir?" he asked Mike.

"Me, four," said Mike. And then ... raucous laughter, again.

The man smiled as he walked toward the kitchen and soon returned with four sodas, four glasses, and four straws.

Soon the car was full of chattering and laughing kids and then a number of waiters wheeled in carts piled with plates of food, each covered with a silver lid. Our waiter pulled the cart to our table and set a plate in front of each of us and then lifted the lids to expose our breakfast. Each plate contained two eggs, two pieces of bacon, two pieces of toast, and a little paper cup filled with jelly. The eggs were what they called sunny side up but they looked almost raw as they jiggled around on the plate with the motion of the train.

"Cripes, these eggs are raw!" Dewey bellowed.

The waiter's smile vanished and he looked worried.

"Dewey, shut up! They're okay," I said.

"I'm not eatin' raw eggs," he said.

The waiter said, "I can take them back and have them cooked

more.

Dewey handed his plate to him. He looked at the rest of us.

"Uh, could you cook ours a little longer, too?" Chick said, and we all handed him our plates. He smiled and took them to the kitchen and in a few minutes he returned; eggs were cooked through, alright! Hard as rocks, but that was the way we liked them.

"Thanks," Dewey said, and we all echoed words of gratitude.

The man grinned and served the others.

We finished our breakfast, went back to our car, and began watching the scenery go by. Soon the hills and woods, common to our part of the world, began to disappear and big buildings and cities were appearing. The landscape became flatter as we traveled into Illinois and approached Chicago. There were buildings and skyscrapers all over the place-quite a change from our town where the tallest building was the hotel which stretched up three stories. We pulled into the train station and the sisters herded us off the train and down the aisles between the loud locomotives coming and going. There must have been 50 trains in the station and diesel fumes, steam, and noise. We hustled out of the station and into the terminal where the sisters ushered us onto a waiting bus.

We had our noses pressed to the glass as we went through downtown Chicago, craning our necks to see the tops of the huge skyscrapers.

"Wow! Holy Cow! Look! Look!" We were awestruck. We drove through streets that weaved around hundreds of impressive buildings until the bus pulled up to the Shedd Aquarium. Sister Henry stood in the front of the bus and gave instructions as to our behavior inside the building. She might as well have been talking in Latin, like Father Lewandowski did in mass, because we weren't listening. We piled off the bus and began our tour of the aquarium. It was an immense building and there were tanks and tanks of fish, from little, brightly-colored ones to huge sharks; even some small whales. Dewey and I were looking at the sharks and he put his mouth against the glass and blew so his mouth got real big and his lips stretched out. I was laughing at him and saw Chick get a worried look as Sister Arsenia came up behind him and whacked him on the back of the head. "Hey, you dummy," he said, as he turned. "Oops! Sorry, Sister." Sister Arsenia made him get paper towels from the washroom to clean off the glass. After she walked away, Dewey was grumbling that there was surely an aquarium employee who was in charge of cleaning the glass, and he didn't think it was fair that he be made to do it. In fact, he said, he might be taking away some guy's job, causing him to be fired because he didn't have any work to do. Only Dewey could think of something like that.

We spent a couple of hours in the aquarium and then we headed to the Museum of Science and Industry. This place was full of cool things-like real airplanes hanging from the ceiling, and a mock coal mine that seemed like a real mine. Sister Henry told us that we were free to explore but we must be on the bus at two o'clock to go to the next museum. Chick, Dewey, and I made our way through miles of the place and had a great time discovering many extraordinary things. Of course, Dewey found a snack bar and we had to stop for ice cream and soda so he would have energy to keep looking. We kept a close watch on the time and were back at the bus with a few minutes to spare.

Off we went down the canyons between the tall buildings again and we stopped in front of the huge Museum of Natural History. It took up a whole city block and there were busses parked all around it. Sister said we had to tour this museum as a group because it was so large so we followed her like a string of baby ducks. Upon entering the building, we were captivated by the huge dinosaur skeletons. Dewey stood there, gaping at them, and he blocked the door until Sister Arsenia smacked him on the head.

We walked up to a mammoth set of bones and stood there without talking. It seemed that the skeleton would come alive if it heard us.

"Do you think there is anything like that around our home?" Dewey whispered.

"Yeah, Dewey. I saw one down at Gutweiler's the other day; did I forget to tell you?" I whispered. Chick burst out laughing and Sister gave us the kind of look we usually got for fooling around in church.

"Come along, children, and don't stray behind or you'll get lost," Sister Henry said, as she waved us toward her.

"Come along, children; don't get lost," Dewey mimicked. We went for miles through the museum and soon I had no idea which way was which. We were in a display area with stuffed fish and whale exhibits that made them look as if they were swimming. I was fascinated by a gigantic blue whale as big as a school bus and I stood there mesmerized, imagining it alive in the ocean. It was the biggest swimming creature I had ever seen.

"Do you think that crappy fishing pole of yours would land this one, Dewey?" I said. I turned to verify that my insult to his fishing tackle had been duly-noted and found that I was alone! I checked both ways in the big room and there was no one there but me. I took off running for the door, peered into the hall, but I saw no one I recognized. But, this was the door through which we had entered, so I ran to the other end of the room and went out that door. Nobody was there! Now I panicked. I had no idea where the rest of the kids and the sisters had gone, so I began running up the halls, looking for somebody I knew. All I saw were strangers who looked at me like I was lost. I was lost! I ran and ran and began sweating and panting like a dog in August.

Suddenly I was in the big room with the dinosaur skeletons.

There were four entrances and I had no idea which door we had entered by, so I ran for the closest one and flew through it. There was no one from my school anywhere to be seen, and there were at least a hundred busses parked end to end as far as I could see around the block. They all looked the same to me so I ran across the sidewalk to the closest one and looked in. It was full of kids I didn't know; so I ran to the next one. It was empty, so I ran to the next, and the next.

I was about half way down the second street of buses when, just as I got to the bus door, Sister Henry stepped out on the sidewalk. I stopped in my tracks, trying to decide if I wanted to make a break for it through traffic and become a homeless kid in Chicago, or face her wrath. Her face was tightly pinched and she grabbed me by the T-shirt.

"Do you realize that everyone else is on the bus?"

"Yes, Sister."

"Do you know how long we have been waiting for you?"

"No, Sister."

"Do you think it's proper for you to keep the whole bus waiting for you?"

"No, Sister."

"Why is it that everyone except you is on the bus and you are out here fooling around?"

I thought for a second on that one. I wanted to say that if they had mentioned to me that they were leaving the whale room, I probably would have been on the darn bus, but they slipped out and ditched me, so that was why I was late. But, my better sense told me to plead for mercy. "I'm very sorry, Sister. I must have been too interested in learning about whales and I didn't see you leave the area."

She looked me up and down and apparently bought my answer because she said, "Get on the bus, and try to behave for the rest of the trip."

"Yes, Sister!"

I was never so glad to see Chick and Dewey, even though they made fun of me for getting lost for the rest of the day. We toured the city a while longer and the bus driver, using a loud speaker, told us about the sites we saw as we traveled. Suddenly, Chick, Dewey, and I were spellbound as we approached Wrigley Field. This was like the most famous place we had ever heard of, and there it was-the home of an actual major league baseball team.

We watched it go by like it was a shrine to the Virgin Mary. There were probably live baseball players behind those walls; the guys whose baseball cards we collected, traded, and guarded like gold. And here we were-so close to them. We watched as the stadium disappeared behind the bus, gazing until we could no longer see it.

Our next stop was China Town. Actually, it was just a part of Chicago that was full of Chinese people and lots of little tourist shops. We had two hours for walking and shopping, so Chick, Dewey, and I looked for souvenirs. I found a fancy tea cup and saucer for mom and chopsticks for my brothers. Chick chose an elaborate silk fan for his mom, and Dewey bought a Chinese straw hat that looked like an upside down funnel. "This will make a cool fishing hat," he said. Chick and I just shook our heads; poor Dewey had finally lost his mind. Then we went to a Chinese restaurant for our meal. We did not know what we were eating but the food was tasty and there was plenty of it for not much money. Then we met up with the bus again and loaded up for our last pass through the city.

We finally arrived at the train station and we piled on the train for the trip home. Soon it was dark and the lights of the city faded away into the night and the distance. Lights of farms and small towns began to dot the landscape and the car quieted down as, one by one, kids drifted off to sleep. Dewey, Chick, and I, still awake, were talking about Wrigley Field. Even Sister Henry and Sister Arsenia had fallen asleep. Arsenia was slumped over with her mouth hanging open and drool was running out while she snored away. We gingerly stepped through the car to the back door, crossed to the next car, and then to the next. We reached the caboose and found it empty. We stepped out onto the little plat- form and noticed an electric light hanging on it, like a taillight. We breathed in the night air as the wind swirled around us and we watched the tracks disappear behind us. Home was just ahead and the big city was farther and farther behind us.

"Would you like to live in Chicago?" Chick said.

"Naw! Not me," Dewey said.

"Me, either," I said. "I didn't see any place to fish except Lake Michigan, and that looks like a place where we would really get into trouble." The three of us laughed and then we just stood there, getting closer and closer to home, where we didn't have to worry about getting lost. It was a good feeling to know our moms would be waiting for us, and we knew our beds would feel good that night. It had been a great adventure to visit the big city, but we were small town boys, satisfied with what we had at home. Once we were home, I barely made it from the car to my bed before I was sound asleep.

Play Ball!

There were two home-made baseball fields in town; one on the west side of town, where we played, and one on the east side of town, where the east-side kids played. There was a ball field at the city park where the big kids played but we avoided that one. Our field was on the same block as my house. There were two vacant lots next to my neighbor's house that we had converted into a baseball field the previous year. The area was about a hundred and fifty-feet square and it made a perfect ball field for us. My neighbors, Fred and Mary, mowed the grass when it got too tall for playing ball. They didn't mind us yelling and playing; in fact, they often sat in the shade and watched us. We laid out our bases, home plate, and a pitcher's mound in the back corner of the field near the alley. Then we hauled in dirt, dumped it on the pitcher's mound, and placed a piece of rubber doormat on it for the pitcher's foot. Our bases were seat cushions off old kitchen chairs that we had come across behind the furniture store. They worked well even though they were covered in red vinyl instead of white canvas like you'd see in the major league parks. Home plate was a converted rubber car mat from a car we had found in the junkyard. We used a tin snips to cut it to the shape of an actual home plate. It did the trick, even if it was light blue-not exactly the color of a manufactured one.

There was a sand pit in right field and a couple dozen small pine trees so it made a long-ball hard to field. Fred had planted the trees several years before so we couldn't think of clearing them out. We had to make do by jumping through them to catch fly balls, or by crawling through them, as fast as we could go, to intercept the grounders. There were also sandburs growing in right field and it wasn't uncommon for a base runner passing first base, on his way to second, to get a strip of them thrown at him as he sped by. The street was the home run line, and the Methodist church was across the street in deep right field. The church, with its stained glass windows, was something we thought about whenever a long ball was hit in that direction. Thankfully, few of us could hit well enough to come close to it on the first bounce.

Left field was flat and grassy and well suited for the outfielders. But, it was the worst direction for a long ball to go. Across the street lived the meanest man in town, Verlin Berkamer. He kept an eye on us and whenever we hit a ball into his yard, he picked it up and kept it. Of course, we would yell and scream, but he didn't care. We tried to play during the day when he was at work so we wouldn't have to constantly replace the ball.

Our biggest problem was our backstops. Fred's garage was behind the right side of home plate. Fred's garage had two four paned windows on the ball field side. During the course of the summer, we managed to break every one of them; and some, several times. Then it was necessary to take a time-out to replace them. Fred kept a supply of windowpanes and a can of window putty in his garage and, by summer's end, we were experts at window repair. Chick and I could take out the old pane, clean off the old putty, and install a new one before the other players could get a drink from Fred's water hose.

The backstop on the left side of home plate was also a garage. The door, which faced the ball field, had six small windows in a line. These panes were also replaced frequently and these neighbors, Henry and Mary, likewise kept a supply of panes and putty for us. Mary, or Grandma Stadele, as we called her, often treated us to cookies during the game. We took special care to do a good job on their window repairs. Fortunately, for the most part, we had pleasant neighbors with a good sense of humor who enjoyed our games, except for old Verlin.

Dewey was in right field because he was our slowest guy and there generally wasn't much business in right field. Chick was our second baseman, and Dougie played shortstop. My neighbor, Charlie, was our pitcher. He had a fastball that would whiz by so quickly that you could barely see it. We figured he would be a professional baseball player someday. "Sticks" was the center fielder. He was the tallest kid on the team, weighed the least, and had arms and legs that looked like sticks; hence, the nickname. "Rocket" was our left fielder. Next to Dewey, he was the slowest guy on the team; so, of course, he was "Rocket." Dennis was our third baseman, but we called him "Hounee," for no reason other than everyone had a nickname and he seemed to be a "Hounee." Fred's grandson, Tommy, was catcher, and I was first baseman. If someone was missing, we usually moved Dewey into the spot, leaving right field undefended. That was most of the time—even if Dewey was there. He lost interest in the game easily and would lie down in the shade next to a little pine tree and take a nap if things were a little slow. Sometimes he would collect a supply of sandburs for an attack on a poor base runner.

Sandburs grew in abundance in our town. The ground was sandy and they were tough little plants, surviving where nothing else could. The plant looks like a clump of grass, but it sends up a shoot with seeds, or in this case, burrs. The seed shoot is a stiff spike with pea-size burrs that bear about a thousand sharp, protruding, tiny barbs. I suppose Mother Nature designed them that way so they would attach to the fur coats of animals and be distributed across the landscape where they would produce new plants. It was a very clever idea. But we used them as weapons. If the spike was broken off when the sandburs were green, they adhered to the stem and you could throw the works at a passerby and the burrs would stick in the hide like a row of daggers. If you threw them with force, they would become buried and most difficult to remove. Individual little burrs had to be pulled out and they stuck in the fingers of the victim, causing even more pain and discomfort. All in all, they made a delightfully effective weapon. And they were plentiful, and free.

We played baseball almost every day, taking turns batting

and having infield practice. About three days a week, we played against the east-side team. Their field was an entire vacant block. They had a real backstop, made of poles and chicken wire, which worked much better than the garages we used. But they didn't have a street for a home run fence, so they used flags tied to sticks for home run lines; a crumby setup compared to ours. Somehow, they had acquired real bases and a home plate, and their pitcher's mound was a little better than ours. Still, we were proud of our field, despite the sandbur patch in right field.

Most of the kids on the east-side team were from St. John's but they had some public school kids, too. A couple of them were eighth-graders and pretty good ball players. They even had one ninth-grader who was almost a professional compared to the rest of us. We met at one of the ball fields about every other day in the summer and we played a game that just kept going, from day to day, and week to week. We never kept score, but we played and played until we got tired of it, or until the sun became too hot. Then we headed to the Gosey for a swim.

Most of us weren't allowed to swim in the river, but the Gosey technically wasn't the river. Where the stream from Gutweiler's Lake emptied into the river, there was a protruding finger of land that made a small lagoon. That was the Gosey. We felt it was safe to swim there as long as we didn't stray past the finger of land into the main river.

It was a great life in the summer. Sleep late, go fishing, go swimming, or play ball-every day. Some days we had a full team; other days we were a few players short, depending on how well the bluegills happened to be biting.

A few days after our trip to Chicago, the east-side guys came to our field for a game. Of course, there were the usual insults to our red bases and floor-mat home plate, but the game started and soon we were enjoying a good afternoon of baseball. One of the east-side eighth-graders was up to bat and he hit a long fly ball into deep right field. As usual, Dewey didn't even come close to catching it and the ball cruised over his head, bounced on the pavement, and sailed through one of the basement windows of the Methodist church. The game was brought to a halt and we hurried to the church to assess the damage. We peered into the church basement through the broken window and saw our ball resting on one of the tables in the church kitchen; sitting in the little basket on the center of the table where the napkins were kept.

"Well, that ball's gone for today," Dewey said. "Let's go swimming."

"We've got another ball," said one of the east-side team members, so we ran back and resumed the game. On the next pitch, their batter hit a line drive out of the park and into mean, old Verlin's yard.

"Holy cow!" Chick said. "There goes our other ball."

"I'll get it," said one of the east-side kids who didn't know about old Verlin. He took off across the street, entered Verlin's yard, and grabbed the ball. Verlin came flying out of his house, yelling at him as he hurried back to the ball field. Of course, we had to shout back, and soon there was a major melee going on between a mean old man and a dozen and a half kids. He was standing on the curb, threatening to call the police and we told him, well—we told him a lot of places he could go, and things he could do, that were not particularly pleasant.

Next we mounted our bikes and rode back and forth in front of his house, yelling at him and calling him names. He stood there, shaking his fist at us, using the word jail. I don't know how long the racket kept up. Suddenly he retreated to his garage and came out swinging a long pole at us as we passed by. Now we were having a great time dodging the pole and yelling insults at him until Chick got too close and Verlin stuck his pole into Chick's front wheel spokes. Chick's bike came to an abrupt stop and he flew over the handlebars and landed on his head, in the street. That did it! We piled off our bikes and headed toward Verlin. He backed up and ran into his house. We were attempting to remove the pole from Chick's wheel spokes when

Mr. Audetta, the town policeman, drove up.

"You boys picking on Mr. Berkamer?" he asked.

"No, sir. We were minding our own business and he came out here yelling at us and he tossed this pole into Chick's bike wheel," Dewey said.

"And why was he yelling at you?"

"Don't know. We were just playing ball," Dewey said, as innocently as possible.

Just then, Verlin came out, bellowing that he wanted us arrested and thrown in jail.

"Hold on, there," Mr. Audetta said. "These boys said you started it."

Verlin came unglued, complaining that we play ball and make a lot of noise and trespass on his property. Mr. Audetta looked at me, questioning if that was true.

"Well, we just play ball. Kids need to yell when they play ball.

We only go over there to retrieve our ball if it's hit across the road. Besides, he has kept about a dozen balls of ours."

Mr. Audetta became interested. "You have baseballs that belong to these boys?" he asked old Verlin.

"If they come into my yard, they're mine," Verlin said.

"And what are you going to do with them?" Mr. Audetta asked.

"Keep 'em."

"What for?"

"So they can't play ball."

Well, Mr. Audetta didn't like that answer and you could see he was getting irritated with old Verlin.

"Well, Mr. Berkamer, here's what we're going to do. You get the baseballs that belong to these boys and give them back. Then, go into your house and stay there. Furthermore, when these boys play ball, you stay in your house, and don't come out. When I drive by, if I see the boys playing ball, and if you are in your yard, I'll take YOU to jail for harassing them. You got that?"

Verlin stood there looking rather stupid. He went to his

garage and came out with a pail of baseballs and dumped them on the ground. Then he opened his mouth as if to address Mr. Audetta but he must have changed his mind, so he turned and went into his house. We let out a huge cheer and scrambled to pick up the baseballs.

"Now, you guys listen up, too," Mr. Audetta said. We stopped dead in our tracks and listened. "You boys play as quietly as you can, and if a ball goes into Verlin's yard, get it, and get back as fast as you can. Don't tramp in his garden or step on his flowers, or anything else, for that matter. Okay?"

"Yes, Sir! Thanks, Sir," we said, almost in unison. Mr. Audetta smiled and climbed into his car.

"Now you have balls to last you all summer," he said. "Have fun, boys." And he drove away.

We picked up our bikes and one of the guys took care of Chick's bike since he was injured. We headed back to the ball field and continued the game. Old Verlin must have been scared off because he never bothered us again. We had a supply of balls that would last us for years to come. After that, we always went out of our way to wave and say hi to Mr. Audetta as he went by. Sometimes he would park his car on the street by the Methodist church and watch us play. He must have liked watching baseball.

War Games

During the summer, we occasionally took time out from fishing and baseball to play Cowboys and Indians or GI's and Germans. Not that we had anything against either one of our make-believe enemies, but someone had to be the bad guys. We took turns taking sides.

A few of the guys had toy guns, or bows and arrows, but generally we used a stick for a gun, and a dirt clod for a hand grenade. This arrangement worked well along with the sound effects we made as we attacked. After a few weeks of make-believe, Chick showed up one day with a water pistol. Of course, we each began a campaign of pestering our moms for money to buy a water gun, too. It didn't take long until we were all sporting water pistols of one sort or another which made the game more fun since you could see that you had scored a hit by the wet spots on shirts and pants.

Then Dewey came up with the idea of water balloons and the game took a new twist. Now we could not only shoot at each other, but we could hurl water grenades at the enemy. The possibilities were endless and the water made the game gloriously wet and muddy. The water balloons were also tossed at unsuspecting friends as they stood in their yards, or up town on the sidewalk, minding their own business. We would ride by on our bikes and pelt them before they knew what had hit them.

By the middle of the summer, the water weapons had become old, but the sandburs were peaking, and they became the weapon of choice. Sandburs grew everywhere. At least they grew wherever the area was not mowed. Vacant pieces of land always had a few sandbur plants; they grew in the right-field area of our ball park, along the roadsides, and in other neglected places. One block from my house was a wooded area with a fairly steep hill that we used for sleigh riding in the winter. The wooded area was also great for our mock battles in the summer.

We would divide into teams. One team would hide near the hill and the other team would come in for the attack. Each person, armed with a bouquet of sandbur stems, would run at his opponent, throw the stalk at him, and then retreat as quickly as possible. The sandburs would become buried in the flesh and hurt like heck. This was fun, unless you were on the receiving end. The sandbur season didn't last long because the plants dried out, the burrs fell off, and they became useless for warfare.

Luckily, Chick came up with a solution for a new weapon when he went to the A & W. He ordered a thick malt. Special plastic straws were provided because regular paper straws collapsed with the extra sucking effort required to draw the malt up to the mouth. Chick happened to keep his straw one day, and when he got home, he noticed that a dry navy bean would fit in it perfectly, and if you blew through the straw, the bean shot out like a bullet. We were sitting in the shade near the ball field when he rode up on his bike. His cheeks were stuffed, like a chipmunk's, and a straw was dangling out of his mouth. We looked up, reprimanded him for being late again just as he aimed the straw at us and delivered a volley of wet beans. We were taken by surprise, and by the time we had figured out what had happened, he was reloading and gave us a second round. It was a delightful new weapon and we couldn't get to the A & W fast enough to buy a malt and obtain our own shooters. The bean shelf at Kalscher's Market was empty in a day. We had a new and wonderful weapon for our war games.

One day we decided it would be a great joke to launch a sneak attack on the east-side baseball team members with the bean shooters. We filled our pockets with beans, grabbed our ball gloves and caps, and pedaled to their field. They had just begun their practice. This wasn't a game day so they were wondering why we showed up and they came over to us. As they got within range, Dewey yelled, "Attack!!!!" and we rallied together and hit them with mouthfuls of beans. They were bombarded mercilessly with beans and fell to the ground in a heap, yelling like madmen. We sped out of there, feeling proud of ourselves for our successful surprise mission.

We heard nothing from the east-side guys for several days so we decided they were afraid to attack us. It was a super hot day. We had knocked off baseball practice early and rode our bikes to the Gosey for a swim. It was far enough from the main road that no one ever ventured down there except us, so we usually felt safe skinny-dipping. It took but a moment to pull everything off and jump into the water. No one was shy, and no one cared if we were swimming naked, so we did it all the time. Additionally, we didn't have to go home with wet shorts or a wet swimming suit and explain to our mothers why we were wet. The river was off limits, and the Gosey was pushing it, as far as the rule went. It was almost part of the river, but we reasoned somehow that as long as water from Gutweiler's Lake flowed in there, it was part of the lake and not the river. I know, it was a stretch, but we managed to convince ourselves and that made it our favorite swimming hole.

We were swimming and screaming and laughing. Then Dougie shouted, "Hey, look! Those guys took our clothes!" And sure enough, there were a couple of east-side kids running down the trail toward town with their arms full of shorts, T-shirts, and shoes. We swam in and took off after them, calling them names and hollering threats. When we were halfway down the trail, the rest of the east-side guys jumped out from behind the bushes and pounded us with beans from their newly-purchased bean shooters. We were in a fix: no bean shooters, no beans, and no clothes! We turned and ran for the water and swam out of bean range. The east-side guys were swollen with pride as they shot beans at us from the bank. We used our only defense-our mouths-and shouted useless threats at them. Finally they ran out of beans and left.

"Now, what we gonna do?" Dewey questioned. "How are we gonna get home, naked?"

"It looks like they left our underwear," Chick said. So we left the water, and sure enough, our underwear was there, in a muddy pile. We sorted through, finding our own, and then we mounted our bikes for the long and humiliating ride through town. It must have been quite a sight-nine almost-naked boys riding down the street in mud-streaked underwear. We arrived at the ball field and found our shoes and clothes in a pile on the pitcher's mound. We jumped off our bikes, picked through the stuff, and dressed, thankful that they hadn't thrown our clothes in the river, or something worse.

Now, we had to retaliate, or suffer the indignity of being the joke of the town for the rest of the summer.

"We have to really make them pay," said Chick. "Let's think of something we can do that they'll never forget."

We agreed the payback had to be something catastrophic, and it had to be delivered quickly. We went home to think and to find ammunition.

The next day we congregated at the ball field and we each brought something for the attack. Chick had the ultimate bean shooter. He had cut off the ends of his mom's fly swatter and the result was a plastic tube, about two feet long, capable of delivering a speeding kidney bean. It was like a grenade launcher instead of a bean shooter. Kidney beans were twice the size of regular beans and would hurt twice as badly. Dougie had a pail of overripe tomatoes that he had "borrowed" from a neighbor's garden. I had water balloons but, instead of water, I had filled them with pickle juice and vinegar. The others had contributed such things as ripe cucumbers, squash, and other nasty stuff. We were ready for the attack. Dewey rode in, late as usual, and he had a big grin on his face. He was handling a sack very carefully. When he approached us, he smiled, and opened the bag to reveal his treasure. It was full of eggs. "They're rotten," he said. "I got them from behind the grocery store. They're the ones that don't sell."

Mr. Kalscher bought eggs from farmers and checked each one with a light to see if it was okay before he sold it. Eggs that weren't clear were thrown away, sometimes remaining for a while in the hot sun before they were collected by the trash men. They got very stinky and nasty in a short time. We were proud of Dewey!

We sent Dougie on a scouting mission. When he returned, he reported that the east-side guys were practicing and all were accounted for. That meant they didn't have spies out. We hopped on our bikes, rode to their side of town, and parked in an alley about a block away. We hid our bikes by a lilac bush behind a garage and worked out our plan. The idea was for Dougie to ride by the ball field and call them names and shoot a few beans at them; then take off as fast as possible. In this way, he would lead them into a dead-end alley. As they passed us, we would attack from behind and they would be at our mercy. It was a good plan.

We divided up the produce and eggs and stink bombs and we hid behind bushes and trash cans and Dougie took off to initiate the attack. Soon we heard screaming and cussing coming closer and closer as Dougie flew by on his bike.

"Ha! He rode into a dead end!" somebody shouted.

"Get him! Make him pay!" The east-side guys came flying by, dust billowing; then, tires screeching to a halt.

Dougie was off his bike, running across the yard when, suddenly, a stink bomb hit one of their guys in the head. That was the signal to attack.

"Yiiieeee!! Attack! Attack!" We threw everything we had at them. They were still on their bikes, trying to ride back to safety, but we pelted them with eggs and stink bombs and beans. Soon they abandoned their bikes and tried to hide behind each other, using their bikes as shields. We kept up the attack until the ammunition ran low and they were pretty well beaten. As the attack slowed, they ran down the alley toward the street, and we let them go. They were plastered with tomato juice, vinegar, rotten eggs, and red welts from kidney beans shot at close range. "High fives" were traded among us. Then we got on our bikes, each one picking up one of the abandoned bikes of the east-side guys. We rode slowly, holding the handlebars of the confiscated bikes, and headed toward the river. When we got to the Gosey, we took off our shoes and clothes and we each took one of the eastside guys' bikes and dragged it into the water, across the Gosey, parking them on the opposite side.

We waded back, put on our clothes, and returned to town. The guys had seen us going in the direction of the river with their bikes so we knew they would eventually head there. We rode around behind them and inched up to the riverbank just as they were emerging from the water on the other side of the Gosey. Chick and Dougie crawled out, gathered up their clothes, and crept back. Then we melted into the woods and found our parked bikes.

Suddenly, you could hear a lot of yelling and shouting as they realized their clothes were missing. "Let's get out of here," Dougie said. We rode to their ball field, piled their stuff neatly on the pitcher's mound and left a note for them: How about a game tomorrow; our field, two o'clock: truce?

Soon there came nine naked boys riding as fast as they could pedal toward the ball field. We hadn't been as charitable as they had been since we had taken everything-even their underwear! They dressed, and then they gathered around to read the note. We saw them talking and then one of their guys waved and made the "okay" sign. All was well.

We had proven that we were not easily outdone. I guess that's why we never kept score in the ball games. Had we done so, we would have taken it too seriously, and that would have taken the fun out of it. At any rate, it had been an exciting few days.

The Haunted House

My friends and I received weekly allowances. The amount varied from kid to kid but it always seemed that the other guys got more money than I did for doing less work. We all complained about our pocket money, but, in reality, we each received about the same amount. The trouble was it never seemed to last the week. Allowance was to cover movies, candy, and summer entertainment. But if we bought soda, ice cream, and baseball cards, there wasn't anything left for movies and popcorn. We had to find ways to supplement our income.

Dewey came up with the perfect enterprise. His dad owned a bar and supper club and if patrons bought beer and soda to take home, there was an additional charge for the bottle. When bottles were returned, the deposit was returned to the customer. It was called cooperage. All bars and grocery stores charged this fee and many bottles went home with customers each week. Often people would consume the beer or soda on the way home and toss the bottles into the ditch. That became the source of our extra spending money. We would ride our bikes toward a neighboring town and collect the strewn bottles. When we got as far as we wanted to travel, we returned on the other side of the road, still searching for bottles. On a good day there would be two or three dollars worth of bottles which helped our finances immensely. Small pop bottles and beer bottles were worth three cents each. Large quart bottles were worth a nickel but they were not as plentiful, probably because more people saved them, and because they broke more easily when tossed from car windows.

We had wire bike baskets on our bikes and, on a good day, we could fill them up. Then we hauled them to Dewey's dad's bar. He counted them and we collected the money. We shared the profit evenly unless we were buying something for the ball field or an overnight camping trip. There were five main roads coming into town and if we alternated between them, leaving a week or so between passes, we would generally fare well.

One particular day, we were riding to Blue River, a town about five miles away. We usually went halfway but on this occasion we intended to go the entire distance because we were planning a weekend camping trip and we needed a good supply of pop and chips for the outing. Dewey and Chick were ahead of Dougie and me, loading up a good find of bottles they had located in a ditch. Dougie and I passed them. Then I spotted a quart beer bottle and stopped to pick it up. Dougie rode on. Soon the three of us caught up with him. He was waiting for us.

"Do you know where this sandy road goes?" he asked, as he pointed to an overgrown path that disappeared into the woods.

"Nope. I've never been down this far before," I said.

"Let's take a look," said Dewey, who was always looking for a loophole when it came to work.

"Yeah, let's," said Chick who was always looking for something to explore.

"Okay, here we go!"

We snaked down the wooded, winding road. Hot and dry conditions caused the dust to billow behind us as we moved farther from the highway. Suddenly we came to a clearing and an old house. It had once been white but the paint had faded to gray. The siding was buckled and dried out. Windows were broken and the front door was standing open. The rusty tin on the roof was buckled. Weeds and brush had grown up around the house and the place looked like it had been abandoned years before.

There was a small shed and an outhouse behind the house, but the strangest thing of all was the fence. It had been constructed of sticks and branches that were piled and woven together. It surrounded the entire yard and ended in front with a wooden gate. The fence was about four feet tall and it reminded me of movies about Africa where people built fences around their villages to keep out lions.

"What the heck kind of animals did they have in here?" Dougie asked.

"Maybe pigs or something," said Chick.

"Or, maybe spooky people like you see on Twilight Zone, or a monster of some sort," Dewey said. "I saw a show that had a house like this that was full of nasty-looking people who were from outer space or somewhere."

"Oh! Sure! Those weird people on the Twilight Zone are real and are running loose these days," I said. We all laughed at Dewey and his big imagination.

"You never know. They could be real and maybe this is a place where they were kept in pens, like animals," lamented Dewey. "And I suppose this happens to be one of those places?" I asked.

"Could be! You don't know," Dewey said.

We laughed at him and decided to take a look. There was a dead tree, standing like a scarecrow with its naked branches stretched toward the sky, in the front yard. A worn out tire was attached to a rope hanging from one of the big branches. There was a bare spot in the dirt where swinging feet had made a depression. We walked behind the house and jarred open the door of a shed that was full of trash, tin cans, broken furniture, and tattered clothes. Dewey took a stick and began digging in the trash, searching for pop or beer bottles, and the rest of us turned to go. Suddenly, Dewey let out a scream and plowed into us as he flew from the shed. "A dead baby! Oh, no! There's a dead baby in there!" He was blubbering and shaking. We mustered up the courage to peek into the shed. Chick started laughing, went to the trash pile, and picked up the head of an old doll.

"Dewey, you dummy!" he said. It's a doll."

"A what?"

"A doll. It's a toy doll's head." Chick tossed the head at Dewey who dodged it and then carefully looked it over on the ground.

"It looked like the real thing when I uncovered it."

We laughed at Dewey. Now it was time to check out the house. Perhaps the Twilight Zone people were big pop drinkers, leaving us a fortune in bottles. The boards on the front porch creaked and groaned as we stepped on them.

"Dewey, you go first. If they hold you, we're safe," said Chick.

Dewey stuck out his tongue at Chick.

The house was empty, except for the worn curtains hanging on the windows and the strewn-about magazines and papers. Out-of-date wallpaper had peeled off the walls and the ceiling was marred with brown, water-stained spots. As we passed through the house, room after room, I noticed that it was getting dark outside. I looked at the sky and spotted an approaching ominous black storm cloud.

"Uh, oh! We're gonna get wet," I said. "We either gotta make a run for home or stay here till the storm passes."

"Let's stay here," Chick said. "Yeah. This is cool," said Dougie.

"I think we should go. There might be the ghosts of Twilight Zone characters lurking here and they might not want us hangging out in their house," said Dewey. We chuckled and decided to ride out the storm in the old house.

As the wind picked up, the curtains fluttered and billowed.

The papers that were lying on the floor were stirred as the lightning crashed and the thunder rumbled. It was scary. The first drops of rain made a loud thumping sound on the tin roof. Soon there was a cloudburst and the sound changed to a constant drumming. Then it became very dark. Dewey was terrified so Chick, taking advantage of this, sneaked up behind him, grabbed him, and scared him half to death.

Meanwhile Dougie was exploring the house and called out, "Hey! Come here. I found something."

"Oh, no," Dewey said, "I'm not going anywhere. You guys are trying to scare me."

Chick and I went to Dougie. Dewey stayed put for about half a minute and then joined us. "You guys wait up. Don't leave me alone," he said.

"Check this out," Dougie said, pointing toward the ceiling in the bedroom. There was a rope dangling from a trap door. "I'll bet that's where the last of the Twilight Zone folks were kept," he said, winking at Chick and me.

"Come on, you guys. Let's go. I've seen enough," Dewey said.

"It's pouring rain, Dewey! Let's see what's up there," Chick said.

Chick got on his hands and knees and Dougie climbed on his back, reached up, and grabbed the rope. Then he jumped down, pulling the rope with him. As he hit the floor, the trap door popped open and a set of stairs slid part way down.

"Wow! Stairs," Dougie said. "Pull them down." We gave a yank and a set of stairs slid down a little track, accompanied by a cloud of dust. It looked as black as night behind the opening.

"Who's first?" I said.

"I'll go," Dougie said. He climbed up and cautiously peered into the attic. Then, a scream! "Ah! No!" He frantically backed down the ladder. Dewey turned and ran into the front yard, into the pouring rain, as the three of us stood laughing in the doorway. "Psycho!" Dougie said.

"That wasn't nice!" Dewey said, as he ran back into the house. "You scared me again!"

We had another good laugh on Dewey. Dougie climbed the stairs again. "Wow! There's an ancient rocking chair up here."

"Anything else?" Dewey whispered.

"Nothing but a lot of dust," Dougie said.

"Let me see," I said, and Dougie came down and I took my turn.

There was a lone rocking chair in the middle of the attic. It looked strange to me and I was trying to figure out what was wrong when Chick pulled on my leg and motioned for me to come down so he could climb up. When he came down, Dewey reluctantly climbed up. Chick gave the ladder a shake.

"Oh, you guys are so immature," he said. He looked at the

chair for a few minutes and then said, "Hey, guys. Why isn't there dust on the chair?" Then I knew why the chair had looked funny. The attic and contents were layered in dust, but the chair was shiny and clean, as if it had been dusted, or rocked in recently.

Dewey descended as fast as his legs would go. "I think there's a ghost up there and it rocks in that chair; that would explain the absence of dust," he said. We were contemplating that thought when we heard a creaking sound coming from the attic. It was a steady creak, creak that sounded like someone was rocking in the chair. We looked at each other and had the same idea. We bolted out the front door at lightning speed. Once on our bikes, we peddled down the dark road toward the highway as fast as our legs could pump.

"Hurry up! It could be coming after us," Dewey shouted.

Our tires were throwing mud and the bottles in our baskets were rattling and clanking as we rode faster than the wind traveled.

The storm had passed by the time we hit the highway. We slid to a stop and gazed down the dark road that weaved through the pine trees.

"I ain't going down there again," said Dewey.

"Oh, come on Dewey. You aren't really scared, are you?" Dougie said.

"I didn't see you waiting behind to take another look," Dewey retorted.

"Let's go. We have a great bunch of bottles. We don't need to go all the way to Blue River today. Let's head back on the other side and finish up," I said.

"Yeah! And let's go to the A & W for a chocolate sundae. I think I need one after that!" said Dewey. Good, old Dewey. No matter how bad things were, ice cream made him feel better. But then, a sundae did sound like a good idea.

We Build a Boat, or Two

Dougie and I were fishing at Gutweiler's Lake one day when we came up with a new idea. We thought if we got away from the usual fishing holes, we would attract fish that hadn't seen our baits and, of course, we'd have better luck. Only part of the shoreline was good for fishing because the beaver dams caused the low places to flood and become swampy. In other words, if you kept to the hard ground, you missed out on much of the lake. We figured the big ones were surely in the places we couldn't get to. One day we wore boots and were able to wade along the edges of the lake, casting to new and unexplored waters.

"This is great," Dougie said, as he reeled in a nice bass.

"Yeah! We should have thought of this a long time ago. We could be the best fishermen in town," I said.

Dougie unhooked the bass and let it go since we had previously decided to throw back all fish. Then he cast toward the weed bed. I had directed my trusty, red and white *BassOReno* into a patch of lily pads and I was cranking it back. This was probably the luckiest *Bass 0 Reno* in the whole world. The paint was almost worn off from the teeth of the many northern pike that had taken it. If you cranked slowly, the *Bass 0 Reno* stayed on top and moved along with an enticing wiggle, like a sick, struggling fish; just the right-size meal for a big bass or northern pike. It was about half way back when a huge fish made a swipe at it, but missed. "Whoa! Dougie, there is a huge northern after my bait," I said. I kept reeling, had about three feet of line still out and I was just about to lift my *Bass 0 Reno* out of the water and cast again, when a northern pike, the size of Moby Dick, came out of the weeds open-mouthed and grabbed it. The fish's mouth appeared to be the size of an ice cream bucket and it was lined with long, spike-like teeth. The northern grabbed it with such momentum that he kept coming at me as if he wanted to eat me, too! I let out a yell and ran backwards in the weeds and water while the fish thrashed on top of the water with my lure in his mouth. Then it slapped its tail on the water as it dove back into the weeds. I was standing there, dripping wet, with my fishing pole and a limp line dangling in the water.

"Holy cow! That was a huge one!" Dougie yelled from down the shore.

"He got my favorite *Bass 0 Reno!*" I was furious because the lure cost almost two dollars and this one, particularly, brought good luck, and now it was gone. "Let's go home. I'm tired of fishing," I said.

Dougie knew how special that *Bass 0 Reno* was and he felt sorry for me so he didn't make any jokes about it. "We gotta get a boat so we can get out to those places where the big fish live without being in the water with them," I said. Dougie agreed.

We rode the dirt road back to town and I was feeling pretty miserable. Now I'd have to save up allowance and bottle money to replace the lure, and who knows if the new one would work as well. We were riding past Mr. Schwingle's hardware store when Dougie yelled, "Whoa! Stop! Look at that."

There was a large, empty, wooden crate sitting on the sidewalk behind the store. It was about ten feet long, three feet wide, and three feet deep. "We could make that into a boat," I said, as I looked at Dougie who nodded in agreement.

"No kidding! Let's ask Mr. Schwingle if we can have it," he said.

We parked our bikes, went into the store, and Mr. Schwingle came to greet us. We were regular customers, buying our hooks and sinkers and stuff from him, and we were often there when he uncrated refrigerators. If we helped him, he would give us the boxes for forts and stuff. We asked him if he planned to throw away the wooden crate. He said yes and went on to offer it to us--and to haul it to my house after store hours. We were happy, thanked him, and went to Chick and Dewey's houses to report the good news. We had a boat!

That evening we began working. We decided the box was too tall so we got saws, hammers, and nails, and lopped about one foot from the top of the box. Then we used the wood we cut off to make seats in the boat. It resembled an old-fashioned casket and was slightly odd looking, being square on each end, but we didn't care.

The next day we decided to pool our money to buy putty or caulk to seal up the cracks so the boat wouldn't leak. We soon realized we needed a method of moving the boat through the water. We found a few straight small trees, cut them down, and stripped off the branches. These became our pushing poles. Then we encountered our biggest problem-getting the boat to the lake. We were sitting in the shade, trying to figure it out, when Mr. Schwingle drove up in his pickup truck.

"I thought I'd see how your project is coming," he said. We showed him our handiwork and he seemed very impressed. "How are you going to get it to the lake?" he asked.

"Don't know," Dewey said.

"Nope, don't know," we all chimed in, looking at the back of his pickup.

"Maybe I can give you a lift," he said, smiling. We gave a hearty cheer and grabbed the corners of the boat and lifted it into Mr. Schwingle's truck. Then we piled our bikes on top for the ride to the lake.

When we arrived, we unloaded the stuff and thanked Mr. Schwingle for his help. "You guys try that thing out in the shallow end of the lake."

"Okay, we will," we said, and we started to drag the boat to the bank. Mr. Schwingle drove away, chuckling to himself

The boat settled into the water with about a foot and a half of boat sticking up. "That's good," Dougie said. "Doesn't look like the water will come over the side."

"I wanna ride in the front," said Chick, and he crawled in. "Me, next," Dewey said, and he walked to the other end next to Chick.

Then Dougie got in and I pushed the boat away from the bank and jumped in the back of the boat. Now there was only about half a foot of boat sticking above the water.

"Whew, we better sit still, or we'll take in water," Dougie said, leaning over to see how close we were to the water surface.

"Row! Row!" Dewey said. "Push those poles; swab that deck!"

Suddenly Dewey had become Captain Hook. Dougie and I began pushing with the poles and the boat moved slowly toward the middle of the lake. It wasn't a pretty thing, but we made it to the center of the lake where we never had a chance to fish before and it was great.

"Let's head to the other end," Chick said. So Dougie and I began poling toward the deep end of the lake. We were moving along well when Dewey yelled, "Hey, guys! Water is seeping in!" We looked down and, sure enough, lake water was coming in through the caulked seams!

"That's not so bad," Dougie said. "We can add caulk when we get it back to shore." Dougie had no more than said that when a big crack opened up on the side of the boat and more water began squirting in.

"Uh, oh! That can't be good," Dewey said. And another crack opened on the other side! Now, more water was coming in, like a geyser.

"Head for shore!" yelled Chick.

"Hurry up! We're gonna sink," Dewey said, and he stood on top of the seat. Well, that about did it. When Dewey stepped up, the boat tipped to the side and we took in a few more gallons.

"Dewey--you bonehead! Get down. You're gonna sink us," Dougie yelled.

"I'll get my new tennis shoes wet," Dewey whined.

"You're gonna get more than that wet if we sink," Chick added.

Dougie and I tried to turn the boat toward shore but we were having a difficult time accomplishing that because the boat was filling with water.

"Give me a pole," Chick said, and I handed him my pole and he was able to turn us. Just as we were pointed in the new direction, the boat tipped again, and another flood of water came in on us! The boat was now about three-fourths under water and the shore was a long way off.

"We're not gonna make it," I said. "Pole fast, guys, or our boat is going down."

About a minute later, the boat sank downward and we found ourselves swimming. As soon as we were out of the boat, it bobbed at the surface momentarily; then it turned over and plunged out of sight. Luckily, we were all good swimmers, so we made it to shore. We climbed on the bank and gazed at the bubbles coming to the surface of the water as our boat settled into the mud.

"Well, that was a good idea," Dewey said. "And my new tennies are all full of mud. My mom will kill me."

Dougie and I shook our heads at Dewey, and Chick threw a mud ball at him.

"Well, it was a good idea as long as it lasted," Dougie said. "Yeah, it was fun," Chick said.

"We need a boat, one way, or another," I said. I had that unforgettable northern pike on my mind with my *Bass 0 Reno* in its mouth.

We rode our bikes back to town. By the time we arrived, we were coated with road dust that had adhered to our wet bodies. Chick and Dewey turned toward their houses and Dougie and I went the other way to his house. We were sitting in his backyard feeling glum when he suddenly looked up. "You know, I've got an old telephone pole out back that was once a basketball backboard pole. My dad wanted it out of the way so he took it down and the pole is lying behind the garage."

"I don't want to get up in the air," I said. "I want to get to the middle of the lake."

"I know, but listen. We'll cut the telephone pole in half; then, we'll lay the two halves about six feet apart and nail a few boards between them. The inner tubes we use at the swimming hole can be attached to the under side and we'll have a raft. It'll be even better than a boat because it'll be bigger and we'll be higher off the water." I knew right then that I had made a good choice when I made friends with Dougie. He was a genius.

The next day I called Chick and Dewey and told them to meet me at Dougie's house with their tools. We got there about a half hour later and we had a good assortment of saws, hammers, and drills, along with nails and screws that we had borrowed from our dads' workshops. Dougie explained the plan and Dewey and Chick became as excited as I had been.

First, we had to cut the telephone pole in half. We measured it and then began cutting with Dewey's saw. Dewey sawed and sawed and he had barely put a scratch in the pole when he turned the saw over to Chick. Again, a lot of sawing happened but not much pole was cut. I took over; then Dougie took his turn, and we were barely halfway through. "Whew! This is harder than I thought it would be," Dougie panted. "A saw with longer teeth would cut faster." He left and returned with his dad's meat saw that he used to cut up deer. It had long teeth and it worked much better. "We just gotta clean it up and put it back, and he'll never know," Dougie said.

The pole was finally cut in half. We laid the two pieces across from each other and placed a number of boards across them horizontally. We nailed the boards down, making one end even but the other end was jagged because of the varying board lengths. Then, with the meat saw, we trimmed the uneven edge, and our raft was finished. Dougie and I were on one side and Dewey and Chick were on the other and we lifted the raft to check its stability. As we lifted it, one board came loose, Chick dropped his end, then Dewey dropped his end, and in a couple of seconds, the whole thing was coming apart.

"We gotta put it together better," Dougie said. "I have a few 4 x 4 posts that could be nailed to the telephone posts, and then the boards could be nailed to the 4 x 4's. That would give added strength." Dougie was such a good engineer that we all agreed and we tore the boards from the posts. Then we got the 4 x 4's and, since they were already about six or seven feet long, we decided that it would be easier to make the raft longer than to cut them off. We put them in place and drilled a hole in each one. We pooled our money and sent Dewey to Mr. Schwingle's store to buy four long bolts and nuts for connecting the 4 x 4's to the posts. It took much drilling but we finally completed the job and we nailed the boards to the 4 x 4's. We had to use additional boards since the raft's dimensions had grown. Soon, we had our finished product.

"Let's see how strong it is now," I said. Each one lifted a corner and, with a lot of grunting and groaning, we managed to raise it off the ground.

"Wow! This thing weighs a ton," Dewey said.

"No kidding! We're gonna need a lot of inner tubes to keep it afloat," Dougie said.

We also had another problem. How would we get the raft to the lake? We decided to visit Mr. Schwingle and ask if he had an idea since he had helped us with the boat first time around.

We walked into his store and he came to meet us. "How's the boat working?"

"Um ... not so good. It sunk," Dewey said.

"Really? Were you able to get it out of the lake? You were in the shallow end, right?"

"Um ... not exactly. We started in the shallow end but then we went to the deep end and that's where it sank."

"So, where is it now?" he questioned.

"On the bottom of the lake," Dewey said, as if he had asked a stupid question.

"You guys were in it when it went down, I suppose."

"Yeah, but not for long. We had to swim to shore."

Mr. Schwingle just shook his head and chuckled. "I'm glad you guys are good swimmers. So, what are you up to now?" Mr. Schwingle asked.

"Well, you know the bolts Dewey bought a while ago? We made a raft and we want to take it to the lake and get back to fishing," Dougie said.

"A raft? Do you think it'll last longer than the boat?" Mr. Schwingle wondered.

"Yeah. It's much better than the boat and we're gonna put inner tubes under it to keep it floating."

"I see. Well, I hope you have good luck with it."

"Well, we ... well, we kinda wondered if maybe, later, when you close the store, if--maybe, could you help us haul it to the lake?" Chick said.

"Need a lift? Sure. I guess I can do that," he said. "Where is it?"

"In my backyard," Dougie said.

"Okay! You guys be ready at about six-thirty, and I'll help you."

We thanked Mr. Schwingle; then we rode to our homes to eat supper and get the inner tubes. We planned to meet again at Dougie's house.

When Mr. Schwingle pulled up in the alley behind Dougie's house, he looked surprised when he saw our raft. "That's a pretty big raft. I don't think it'll fit in my pickup. I'll go home and pick up my trailer. I'll be right back." We were in such a hurry to launch our raft that we were becoming impatient waiting for him to return. Finally he pulled up with his trailer. With two of us on each side, we were able to lift it up and slide it on the trailer. Then we tossed our pushing poles and inner tubes on the trailer, followed by our bikes, and then we piled on. Mr. Schwingle drove slowly. When we arrived at the lake, he backed the trailer close to the high bank. We removed our bikes and other stuff. Then we edged the raft off the trailer and down the bank. At the shore, we attached the inner tubes and shoved it into the water. Six inner tubes seemed to keep it nicely afloat. Then we climbed aboard what seemed to be a perfect and stable raft. It rode high in the water and gave us much room for fishing and moving around. "Wow! This is great!" Dougie said, as he proudly surveyed his creation. We all congratulated Dougie and thanked Mr. Schwingle for his help.

"You boys be careful, and have fun," he said, as he drove off. We could hardly wait for the maiden voyage but it was already rather late so we decided to tie it up at shore and return early the next morning.

We were extremely happy as we journeyed home. We sang "Row, row, row your boat ... " and "Take me out to the ball game ... " as we rode our bikes. We sang the baseball song because we got tired of "Row, row, row ... " and we didn't know any other lively song. When we got back to town, we separated. Dewey and Chick headed toward their houses and Dougie and I went toward ours. We stopped for a minute at Dougie's house and he said, "I can't wait until tomorrow."

"Me, either! That must be the best raft in the whole world.

We're gonna catch so many fish that we'll easily be the best fishermen that ever lived in this town," I said. We "high-fived" and I went home, dreading the thought of trying to go to sleep, barely able to wait until morning when we would launch the raft.

The next morning, I was up with the sun and got my stuff together for a day of fishing on our new raft. I made peanut butter and jam sandwiches and put them in a plastic bag along with a banana and an apple. Then I grabbed my fishing pole and bait, placing the bait in an old cigar box that usually held my baseball cards. I didn't want to take my tackle box on the raft in case it sank, or in the event that Dewey would manage to kick it overboard.

I arrived at Dougie's house and he and Chick were waiting. They were carrying lunches, tackle, and their fishing poles. Dougie also had a canteen of water so we would have something to drink. Of course, Dewey was late. In about half an hour, Dewey rode up with his pole, already tied with a lure, and a huge grocery sack full of food.

71

"Jeez, Dewey! Are you going for a week?" Dougie said.

"I know I'll be hungry and I don't want to run the risk of going without food," he said. We got on our bikes and headed for the lake.

Our raft was where we had left it. We loaded up the food and gear, then took off our tennis shoes and shirts and left them on the bank. Dougie and I wore Milwaukee Braves baseball caps and Chick had a Philadelphia Phillies cap. He always had to be different. Dewey sported a "grandpa-like" straw hat.

"It's my Huck Finn hat," he said proudly. "If we're gonna be on a raft, I'm gonna be Huck."

"Right, Dewey. But you look more like Aunt Polly," said Chick. We laughed at poor Dewey.

Dougie and I poled and soon we were on the lake with many square yards of new water available to us. "I'll bet nobody has ever thrown a lure in this water before," I said, as I flung my new *Bass o Reno* toward an opening in the lily pads.

"Good shot," Dougie said.

My lure hit the water and it looked like I had thrown a bomb into the lily pads. The water exploded and a huge northern pike shot up like a dolphin in a movie. Then it hit the water and made a huge splash and burrowed back in the weeds.

"Holy smokes!" Dewey said. "Jeez, you got a whale."

"Hang on!" Dougie yelled.

I was holding on for dear life and suddenly the raft began to move across the lake.

"Holy cow! That fish is pulling us!" Chick yelled.

Everyone was talking at once and Dewey was swinging one of the poles, trying to figure out how to stop the raft.

"Dewey, let him pull it. He'll get tired faster that way," Dougie said.

"Get out of my way. Get back! Give me room!" I said, as I tightened the drag on my reel.

We were moving along at a good clip when suddenly the fish turned and came back at the raft.

"He's charging us!" Dewey yelled. The fish came at us and I was reeling up line as fast as I could. He went under the raft and across the lake in the opposite direction. My rod was pulled into the water and I was trying desperately to get it to round the side of the raft.

"Turn us! Hurry! He's gonna break the line!"

Chick was poling and got us about halfway around when the line gave a noisy snap. The raft came to a stop and the four of us stood there, looking at the water.

"That was the biggest northern in the world," Dewey said. "Probably a world record," Chick said.

"Man! That was a huge fish," Dougie said.

I couldn't talk.

"I only got to throw that *Bass 0 Reno* one time," I said. "That was the biggest fish I've ever had on a line."

"Here," Dougie said, handing me one of his *Bass 0 Reno* lures. Good, old Dougie. He was always there to make you feel better. Chick patted me on the back and Dewey offered me one of his sandwiches, and soon we were casting again and having a great time.

We fished all day, consumed all the food and water, and caught a dozen fish. We poled our raft from one end of the lake to the other, believing we had conquered the world. It was one of the best fishing days ever.

As we neared the shore, we were chattering about the good times and what we would do the next time we took the raft out. We rode toward town just as the sun was setting. By the time we got to our homes, it was dusk, and after a bath, we headed to bed--with northern pike in our dreams.

The next day we had a game planned with the east-side guys so we didn't go fishing. But we made plans to do so on the following day. We met at Dougie's house with food and beverage and headed to the lake. We parked our bikes and shoved our shirts and shoes in the baskets and walked over the high bank. The raft was gone!

"What the heck?"

"Not No way! How could anyone have stolen it from this spot?" We were all talking at the same time.

"Look here," Dougie said. The rope that we had used to secure the raft was still around the tree.

"Someone dragged it up the bank," Chick said, pointing to scratch marks in the sand. Sure enough, there were tracks where somebody had lugged the raft up the hill and then the telltale marks that indicated that it had been loaded on a truck or trailer.

"Some thief took our raft!" Dewey said. We stood there, looking down the road as if it had to be there, somewhere! But, it was gone.

"Well," I said, "I hope when they use it, it sinks."

"And may a big whale eat them when they're swimming back," Dewey added. We laughed at Dewey and his ideas.

"Well, it was a lot of fun while it lasted," I said.

"Yeah, we had two boats, each for one day and now we're stuck on the bank again," Chick said.

Well, it had been a couple of enjoyable days with exciting adventures, so what the heck.

"Well, I guess we should hunt bottles and see if we can find more wood for another raft," I said.

"Yeah, and we'll be sure to buy a chain and a padlock next time," Dewey said. We all laughed; Dewey could always say something to make us laugh. Good, old Dewey.

We never did get around to building another raft, and we never found out who stole ours, but that one glorious day of fishing was never forgotten.

Refrigerator Boxes

It started one afternoon when Dougie and I happened by Mr. Schwingle's hardware store as he was taking a new refrigerator out of the cardboard shipping box. Refrigerator boxes were in great demand by all the kids in town. We kept a close eye on the store, trying hard to be on the scene whenever new refrigerators arrived. On this particular day, Mr. Schwingle gladly passed one on to us, and we towed it behind our bicycles to my backyard.

Refrigerator boxes weren't as much a box as a tall, square tube; like a skyscraper without a top or bottom. The bottom of the box was attached to a pallet that was bolted to the refrigerator so it could be moved with a forklift. The metal band, used for securing the load, stayed on the pallet when the refrigerator was removed. The top was the same as the bottom except it was made of cardboard and it also had a metal band. The box was about six feet tall and about three feet square. It had many great uses for kids who had imaginations.

In the winter, a bunch of kids could get inside a box and slide and roll down the sleighing hill. On cold days, the box would last all day; but if it was warm, the cardboard became wet and soggy and useless, but it was great fun as long as it held together.

In the summer we used the discarded boxes for forts and tanks. We would take one box, lay it on its side and bend the sides up to make a big tube. Then we would crawl inside, pretend it was a tank, and we would advance toward the enemy. We played "Soldier." One side was a tank division; the other, a dug-in enemy. The tank guys would roll toward the infantry guys and, invariably, we would roll over them with much screaming and shouting. The infantry guys would be crushed beneath the unstoppable tank. Imagining was great fun. Sometimes we would "crawl" all over town--even crossing streets.

The plan for this particular box involved transforming it into a fort for use in my backyard. Dougie and I laid the box on its side so that one open end was against the end of our picnic table. We built a door for the other end out of laths, beach towels, and blankets, giving it an opening like a tent. More blankets and an old painting tarp were used to incorporate the picnic table into the structure. When it was finished, it looked like a patchwork square igloo instead of a smooth and rounded one. Inside, was a comfortable area with two rooms; one being the box, and the other, the area under the picnic table. Chick and Dewey arrived and we played army all day, inside and outside the new fort.

"Let's sleep here tonight," Chick said.

"Yeah! Let's!" chimed in Dewey. We thought that was a good idea, so everyone went home to get permission and to find food and blankets. I went in to check the plan out with my mom. We all got the "okay" to sleep outside, and soon we were preparing the fort for the overnight adventure. There was room under the picnic table for two to sleep, and two could fit in the refrigerator box. We spread out our blankets, pooled our food, and soon we were having a great time telling jokes and stories, and eating lots of good junk.

"Anybody know a good ghost story?" Dougie asked.

"Did you hear the one about the guy with the hook?" Chick said.

"Yeah, Chick. You've told that one about a hundred times," I said.

"My dad told me about a ghost in this town," Dewey said.

"Oh, sure, Dewey."

"No foolin'. It's a true story. It's about the Gosey."

"What about it?"

"Didn't you guys ever wonder why the Gosey is called the Gosey?" We had to admit that it had never crossed our minds, so we asked Dewey to tell the story. "Well, once upon a time, long ago, there was a kid who lived in France. His name was something like Gosee."

"Something that sounds like a French name," Chick laughed.

"It was a French name. I just can't remember it, dummy: anyway, this kid decided to move to the United States. He left his family, boarded a boat, and arrived in New York City. He couldn't find a decent job so he moved west, finally stopping in Wisconsin. Back in the old days, there was a big dock down where the Gosey is; they loaded ore onto big boats for the trip down the river to the Mississippi. "

"Is there a ghost in this story?" Dougie said.

"I'm getting to that; just wait. This Frenchman gets a job at this dock loading the heavy ore onto the boats. The local guys couldn't pronounce his name properly so they called him Gosey, the Frenchman. One day, while carrying a load of ore, he fell into the river and was not able to escape so he went down to the bottom and drowned. They found his body and buried him there on the riverbank. So, from then on, it was called the Gosey Hole, and they say his ghost is still there, haunting the Gosey."

We were sitting open-mouthed when Dewey finished his story.

"No foolin', Dewey?" I said. "Did you just make that up, or is it for real?"

"My dad told me that's how the Gosey got its name. I don't know why he'd say that if it wasn't so," Dewey said.

"Let's go down to the Gosey and see if he's there," Chick said.

"Yeah, let's," Dougie said.

"When? Now?" Dewey questioned.

"Yeah. Our moms think we're sleeping here. They won't know," Chick said.

We discussed it and decided that if we rode our bikes on the back streets, then cut across the main street at the bridge, no one would see us and we could get to the Gosey undetected. Dewey was the only one who was hesitant.

We slipped out of the fort, got our bikes, and sneaked our way through town toward the river. It was late so there weren't people walking or driving around and we arrived without a problem. We took the sand road to the Gosey and jumped off our bikes at the swimming hole. "Come over here. This is where he drowned," Dewey said, walking toward the high bank. We walked to a bunch of rocks cemented together to form a structure as large as the foundation of a house.

"This is where the dock was, my dad said." Dewey pointed to the foundation.

"I always wondered why this was here," said Chick.

We peered at the block of cement above the riverbank and we could imagine a wooden dock attached to it, projecting out into the river. It would be a good place for a boat to dock to be loaded with ore.

"It's very deep here, too," Dougie said. "Yeah. The deepest part of the Gosey," I said. "Let's go swimming," Chick said.

"What? Now?" Dewey said.

"Yeah. Why not?"

"You afraid the ghost will get you, Dewey?" Chick teased. "Well, no. I don't believe there is really a ghost, but it's dark."

"So what? Come on. Let's go."

We ran to the swimming hole, stripped off our clothes, and hit the water. It was cool at first, but, after we were in for a few minutes, we began to have a great time splashing and dunking one another. Earlier in the summer we had tied a thick, hay rope to a tree branch that hung over the water. We used the rope for a swinging ride over the water, letting go, then splashing down into the water. Dougie and I took off for the swing. Dougie stopped part way to catch a firefly. The air was full of glowing green lights that went off, then back on to a spooky green color. Dougie took the firefly and squished it across his forehead, making it glow.

"Wow! That's cool. You're green," I said. "Put on more."

We both caught fireflies and smeared them on our arms and legs, and on our bellies and faces. Soon we were gleaming like two giant fireflies.

"Let's hide and scare the other guys," Dougie said. "Dewey, come here," we yelled.

"Hey, Chick. See what we got." They came running up the bank, sand and water flying, as Dougie and I hid in the bushes. After they passed us, we stood up quietly and tiptoed behind them. Dougie slipped up behind Dewey, and tapped him on the shoulder. Dewey turned to see two glowing figures. He took off yelling and running for town. Chick knew it was us and laughed as Dewey sped down the road, yelling that a ghost was on his trail.

"Dewey, you numskull! You're naked! Come back!" we yelled.

Dewey almost got to the main street before he realized he was in the nude, stopped, and covered himself with his hands.

"Look at him; he thinks no one will notice him." We were laughing like crazy as Dewey turned and came back.

"Geez, you guys! You're really funny! What if someone would have seen me?"

"They wouldn't have seen much, Dewey," Dougie said, and we laughed again.

The green glow began to fade so we dipped ourselves in the water and scrubbed off the bug juice. Then we sat on the grass to air-dry before putting on our clothes. "That was a good story, Dewey; and it does make sense. Otherwise, why would this place have such a strange name?" Dewey was proud of himself and his fine story.

We dressed and rode our bikes home and settled down in the fort. We ate the last of our food and drank the last pops and then turned in for the night. Then we heard thunder rumbling in the west and soon there were streaks of lightning.

"It's gonna rain," I said to Dougie.

"Yeah. I wonder how long this box will protect us from the rain?" he asked.

"There is a tarp over this part," Dewey said, smugly, from under the picnic table.

A drop or two of rain hit the top of the refrigerator box.

Then-harder and harder--it began to pound and became a downpour. The cardboard part of the fort began to leak and collapse. "Time to abandon the fort!" I shouted to Dougie over the roar of the rain and thunder. We grabbed our blankets and crawled under the picnic table with Chick and Dewey where it was dry. Four boys attempted to be comfortable in a space made for two. Soon the ground was no longer able to absorb the rain, and water trickled in under the edges of the tarp.

"I'm getting wet!" Chick said. "Me, too," said Dougie.

"We better run for my house," I said, and we crawled out through the remains of our ruined fort, ran across the yard in our underwear, and into my house. My mom heard us stomping and banging around in the hallway and got up to see four nearly naked boys fighting over one towel.

"Here," she said, as she handed us dry towels. "I'll get a few blankets and pillows, too." Soon we were bedded down on the living room floor.

"Good night, boys," she said. "Good night, Mom," I said.

"Good night, Mom," Dewey, Dougie and Chick said, chuckling. Mom shook her head and headed back to bed.

"Well, this was a fun night," Chick said, as we laid and listened to the raging storm.

"Yeah, this was pretty cool," I said.

"You know, if we had a real tent, we could sleep out every night," Dougie said.

And, with that idea in our heads, and the storm howling outside, we drifted off.

The Elephant Boys

It had been the subject of conversation for two weeks. The circus was coming to town and we could hardly wait. We had gone on extra bottle-hunting trips, scouring the land until there wasn't a bottle to be found anywhere. We had mowed the lawns in the neighborhood until the yards looked like manicured golf courses, and we had taken other odd jobs to earn extra cash to spend when the circus rolled into town. We didn't want to worry about running out of money, thereby missing something at the circus.

Finally, on Wednesday, the big trucks arrived. Chick flew in on the wind on his bike to inform Dougie and me. We were in my backyard, talking about the death-defying acts we would surely see as well as the wild animals trained by daredevil circus performers that we could watch. We jumped on our bikes to pick up Dewey and then we were off, as fast as we could go, to the vacant lots on the edge of town where the circus was to be set up.

There were dozens of big trucks painted bright red, white, and blue. Some of them held caged animals. There were four elephants, three lions, three tigers, numerous horses, and cages with monkeys and dogs.

"Wow! This is the biggest circus I've ever seen," Dewey exclaimed.

"This is the only circus you've ever seen, Dewey," Chick corrected. We all laughed at Dewey.

The men began to unload the gear from the trucks and to set up tents and, excited as we were, we could barely discipline ourselves to stay out of the way. Soon the guys from the east-side arrived and we sat on our bikes in the shade, watching the spectacle of the circus unfold before our eyes. After the gear was unloaded, the circus workers set up the small tents. The east-side guys became bored and left for swimming, but we stayed,

81

not wanting to miss a thing.

The circus workers knew exactly what they were doing. They set up the tents for the animal cages. They led the enormous, gray elephants, one by one, off the truck and chained them to posts that had been pounded into the ground. Then a man threw leather harnesses on the biggest ones, attached harnesses to the wagons which were stored on a truck, and the strong beasts pulled the wagons off the truck. The man directed them where to go. "Wow! He's got them trained!" I said. We were most impressed. Our training efforts were aimed at our dogs and it was limited to "sit" or "shake a paw." This guy had the ability to make these large critters to do the work of a tractor.

Dougie had had pretty good luck training his beagle, Cookie. He was an overweight beagle who was born hungry. Dougie would take a wiener and make Cookie sit with his paws up. Then he would lay the wiener across his nose. Poor Cookie would sit there, like a nail keg with feet, looking cross-eyed at the wiener. Sometimes he would hold that pose for an hour before Dougie would tell him it was okay to eat the wiener. Then Cookie would flip it into the air, catch it, and "down" it-in two bites. It seemed like a lot of work and patience for such a minimal reward, but Cookie was always ready to do it again and again.

We watched for most of the day as the trucks were unloaded and the vacant lots were transformed into a circus. The men rolled out the big canvas tent that would house the show and soon the elephants were pulling on ropes and raising the tent on big poles. It was almost suppertime when the two worker elephants were led back and chained to their posts. The attendant fed them hay, lettuce, carrots, apples, and oranges. The elephants were extremely hungry and they squealed and stomped when they saw the food. The man called them by name as he fed them and they seemed to like him a lot. "Here, Naomi. Good girl. Here, Shirley," he said to them. "Some for you, Zelda. Come here, Alma." He spoke to each one of them as he fed them,

82

and they wiggled their ears and ran their trunks over him, smelling and feeling him.

"Wow, Mister! Those elephants are really cool," Dougie said. "Yeah! They're my babies," he replied. "I've raised them since they were young so they know me very well."

We were awestruck that someone could have an elephant for a pet. It made our dogs and pigeons and stuff seem puny.

"You guys want to pet them?" he asked. DID we?? Does a one-legged duck swim in a circle?

"Yeah! We sure do," I said.

"Well, come quietly and talk softly to them." We crept forward, slowly approaching the elephants. When we were close, they raised their trunks to sniff and touch us.

"Oh! Oh! I think I'm gonna pee," confessed Dewey.

"Dewey, you dope. Shut up. You'll scare' em," Chick warned. Naomi was sniffing me and Shirley was snuffling Dougie. He reached up with his hand and touched her trunk and she didn't mind. If Dougie could do it, so could I. I touched Naomi's trunk. She looked at me with those elephant eyes and I rubbed her trunk again and she seemed to like it. "Hey guys. Look at this! She likes me," I said.

Chick was petting Zelda and Dewey was watching Alma check out his pants pockets. "She thinks I've got food in here," he said.

"You probably do. Your pockets are likely crawling with crumbs," Chick teased.

It was an incredible experience. All four of us were petting elephants!

"Take some fruit and feed them, if you'd like," the man said, pointing to pails of oranges, apples, and bananas. We each held up a piece of fruit for our elephant and, sure enough, they took it in their trunks and stuck it in their mouths, gave a couple crunchy bites, and then looked for more.

"Oh, my gosh! This is the greatest thing I've ever done," Chick giggled.

"Me, too," Dewey said. Dougie and I were speechless.

We fed the elephants a lot of fruit and then the man said it was time to bed them down for the day, so we thanked him, got on our bikes, and headed home for supper. When we passed the bank, we noticed the time. It was seven-fifty! Dewey said, "It's almost eight o'clock! My mom will kill me for being so late for supper." Eight o'clock! We had been fooling around with the elephants for two hours. We would get killed, but we figured it was worth it.

When I got home, I acted like it was perfectly normal to eat supper at eight-thirty in the evening, but my mom didn't buy it.

"Where have you been?" she scolded.

"I was at the circus grounds and the man attending the elephants invited us to feed them," I replied, as if it was a typical afternoon event.

"You were what? You stay away from those elephants. One of them will grab you and stomp you to mush," she said. Moms could always find terrifying and terrible things to worry about.

"Mom, they're very gentle. They like us." I was just about to explain everything when the phone rang. It was Dougie.

"Hey, can you come out for a little while?" he questioned.

"I don't know. Mom's rather irritated that I was late for supper. Why? What's up?"

"You know that watermelon patch by our worm-digging place? Let's "borrow" a few ripe ones to give to the elephants in the morning." That sounded like a great idea to me, so I asked Dougie to wait a minute and I pestered my mom about giving permission to go to Dougie's for a while. It didn't take much convincing and she gave in. I told Dougie I'd be right there.

Dougie was waiting for me and we rode toward the east side of town, then followed a gravel road that went of town to a dry creek bed running through a rich, black-dirt valley. That was where we harvested our fish worms. We knew a farmer, who lived adjacently, who had about an acre of watermelons growing in the middle of his cornfield. We wouldn't have known about the watermelon patch except that, one day, we had walked up the ditch looking for bigger worms and we spotted it.

It was almost dark, so we rode quietly, stopped at the bridge, and parked our bikes in the tall grass. Then we crept into the creek bed and headed toward the watermelons. We bent over so as not to be noticed and soon we were in the patch, surrounded by watermelons.

"Let's each take two so we can share with Dewey and Chick," I whispered. Dougie nodded and we slinked into the field and began thumping watermelons.

Thumping was how we knew if a melon was ripe. You took your middle finger and tapped it on the side of the melon, in the middle. If it was ripe, it sounded hollow. Dougie and I crawled through the field and thumped until we each found two choice melons. We picked them, putting one under each arm, and headed back to our bikes. We put the melons in our baskets and set off for town.

We took the back streets toward the river and rode down to the Gosey, hiding the melons there in the tall grass. The Gosey was close to the circus so we figured we'd retrieve the melons in the morning. We rode home, feeling quite smug about our evening's work. We never thought it was stealing to take a few melons since the farmer had hundreds of them and he wouldn't miss one or two; or, in this case, four. Besides, it was for a good cause: the elephants.

The next morning we met at Dougie's house and we told Chick and Dewey about our evening's work. Chick thought it was a great idea but Dewey was annoyed that we hadn't invited him.

"Dewey, we'd still be waiting for you to get ready; and besides, if we took you, you would have made so much noise that someone would have discovered us," Dougie reasoned. Dewey stayed irritated but he was also thankful that we had a melon for him, so he recovered.

We collected our melons from the Gosey and set off for the circus. The man who worked the elephants was dragging a hose toward them to water them.

"Hey, Mister," I said. "Do you think your elephants would like fresh watermelon?"

He turned and smiled at us. "And where did you get them?"

"Well, uh ... we just got them," Dougie said. The man grinned and said he thought the animals would love a watermelon treat and he invited us to help him, if we wanted to.

IF we wanted to! What a silly thing to say. We parked our bikes and again tucked the melons under our arms. The elephants seemed delighted to see us and began rocking back and forth, swinging their trunks. We could detect a low rumbling sound coming from their bellies. "Guess that is the hungry sound," Dewey announced.

The man laughed. "That's how they communicate. They're probably saying, "Those fine boys brought us watermelon," the man chuckled.

"Break the melon into pieces and feed it to them piece by piece," he instructed. We each went to "our" elephant, held the pieces up, and watched it grab the food with its trunk, stuffing it into the mouth. There was crunching and slurping and they stuck out their trunks for more. "This is the coolest thing we've ever done," marveled Dewey. We all agreed.

"I wish the east-side guys could see this! They'd be so jealous," Chick bragged.

It would have made the whole thing really cool to be seen by our friends, but we were having such an amazing time, we didn't really care if we were seen or not.

The melon was soon gone and the elephants squealed for more. "Sorry, it's all gone," Dougie told Shirley. The elephant man then asked if we wanted to help him bathe the animals. Bathe an elephant!! Of course we did!! He returned with long-handled brushes and pails and he showed us how to wash an elephant.

First we took off our shirts and shoes and then we filled the buckets with water and added soap. We wetted the elephants down with the hose. They loved it, and so did we. (We squirted water at each other, too, and soon the eight of us were soaked). Then we dipped the brushes in the soapy water and began scrubbing. Suds covered everything and soon the elephants looked like immense, gray piles of snow. We were having a ball and so were our new friends. When they were squeaky clean, we hosed them down.

"You did a great job," the man praised. "You want to exercise them?" This whole thing was getting better and better.

"Sure! What do we do?" Dougie inquired.

He took hold of Naomi's trunk and said, "Naomi, Hup!" And she began walking forward. "Naomi, Back!" The elephant stopped and backed up. "That's how you speak to them. They know you so they'll follow you. Take them to the field and walk them."

The man unchained the elephants and we each chose our favorite one and began to give commands.

"Alma, Hup!"

"Zelda, Hup!"

"Shirley, Hup!"

"Naomi, Hup!"

The elephants walked with us to the vacant field. I don't think our feet touched the ground. It was like we were walking on air. It had to be the most exhilarating thing we had ever done and we all were grinning like the Cheshire Cat as we exercised our mammoth friends around and around the field.

"I'm walking an elephant," Dewey uttered, with a most astonished look. We were four of the happiest boys in our town, if not the whole state; or the whole country, for that matter.

About thirty minutes later, the man asked us to return the elephants to the pen where he chained them. We thanked him for giving us such a neat job and he invited us to return to exercise them again in the afternoon. We promised to return and off we rode to the Gosey for a swim.

We were relaxing in the shallow water, enjoying the coolness, and being very quiet. The experience of being in charge of four elephants had mellowed us. We looked at each other and smiled. If someone had looked in on us, they may have thought we were drunk or stupid. It wasn't typical for us to be so calm.

Finally we recovered from the euphoria of the encounter with the elephants and we resumed our normal behavior of swinging from our diving rope and dunking each other.

We fed and exercised the elephants in the afternoon, as promised. Now, when they saw us coming, they raised their trunks and squealed at us, as if we were long-lost friends.

Meanwhile, the circus people had been setting up the tents and carnival stuff. There were popcorn stands, cotton candy, candy apples, and heaps of other great foods to sample. Plus there were games with teddy bears and other wonderful toys to win. There was a sign on a tent that advertised an incredible monster inside-the strangest animal ever found: a cross between many animals, a freak of nature.

"We gotta see that!" I blurted. Dougie agreed, but Dewey and Chick weren't too interested.

"I'm gonna spend my money on that game and win a teddy bear," Chick announced, pointing at a booth.

"I'm gonna spend my money on food," Dewey added.

Dougie and I were the animal lovers in the gang so we wanted to see the one-of-a-kind freak animal. We would be there first in line in the morning to see everything. It would be a long night as we waited for the circus to get underway.

Next morning we rode to the circus and asked the elephant man if he needed our help. He smiled as we rode up and told us to get to work because the girls were waiting for us. We knew what to do and we fetched the buckets, brushes, and hoses and began scrubbing the elephants. Then we exercised them, just like professional elephant handlers. We were putting on our shoes and shirts when the elephant man said, "Here, you guys have been a lot of help to me. Take these free passes to the big show this afternoon." He handed us four tickets.

"That's great! Thanks, Mister," we said in unison. What super luck! Now we could spend our own money on candy and junk.

We went home to clean up and were back, in line, at noon when the games and stands opened for business as advertised. We made our way around the entire grounds, checking out everything, looking for the best places to spend our money. Chick wanted to playa game with a BB gun because he thought the prize was a big teddy bear-but he only won a Chinese Finger Trap. We made fun of him and his "impressive" prize. Dougie and I were still fascinated by the strange animal so we approached the tent where a man with a microphone was addressing the people who had gathered. He was talking in a dramatic, deep voice. "It was found on the banks of the Missouri River and is thought to be a cross between four or five different animals. It's the strangest animal ever found; one of a kind. No one has ever seen anything so horrible or terrifying before. You'll be amazed!" Dougie and I were standing there with our mouths open, sucking it all in.

"We've gotta see that," I said. Dougie agreed, but Chick and Dewey didn't want to spend the quarter, so they headed to the hotdog stand. Dougie and I paid the man and entered the tent. We were expecting a huge monster in a cage, but all we could see was a tiny wooden crate, with a chicken-wire top, sitting in the middle of the tent. We walked up cautiously and peered over the top. Inside was a bunch of straw, a dish of water, and a little critter that looked much like a raccoon. Its face looked like a coon, but its nose was longer and the tail stood straight up. "Cripes, this is no monster," I said, disappointedly.

"What a gyp!! This is just a freak-looking coon," Dougie complained.

I took a closer look and suddenly it dawned on me. "Hey, I've seen a picture of this in the encyclopedia at school. It's a relative of our coon. But, I can't think of its name."

"That guy was lying to us. He said it was some kind of freak," Dougie fumed.

"No way! I've seen pictures of it. It's from South America, but what is it?" Dougie and I loved animals and were always collecting critters for our home zoos and I knew this was something I had read about. Then it came to me.

"It's a Coati Mundie, and it's from South America," I explained, proud of myself for remembering. "I'm gonna tell the guy what he's got."

We set out to find him. He was talking low and spooky about the strangest creature in the world.

"Hey, Mister! That's not a freak! It's a Coati Mundie from South America," I bragged, thinking the man would be grateful for the information.

"Beat it, kid!"

"But, Mister ... it's not a freak cross. It is a normal animal; a South American coon."

"I said, beat it! Get out of here!" he hissed.

I looked at Dougie and we knew the man was a fraud, making a lot of money with this fake freak.

"Hey, Mister!" He looked down at us. "Either we get our money back or we're gonna squeal the truth to everybody who walks up."

"I told you to beat it!" he exploded.

That did it! Dougie and I stood in front of the tent and yelled out to people that the animal was a Coati Mundie from South America, that the man was a faker, and to save their money. We hollered that out about twice when he motioned for us to come.

"Here, take your quarters, and get out of here!" he said, tossing two quarters at us. We picked up our quarters and shoved them in our pockets.

"Thanks, Mister," we said, smiling smugly. We walked off and quietly spread the information anyway. In an hour, the tent was closed and the man was nowhere to be seen. We saw him later, cleaning cages behind the big tent, and he gave us a nasty look. We smiled and waved to him. We didn't appreciate getting cheated in our hometown.

The afternoon performance of the big show was to start at two o'clock, so we made our way to the big tent, presented our passes, and got good seats in the front row. There were swings and high wires stretched across the top, and festive circus music was coming from a big calliope at the end of the big ring. Soon the bleachers were packed with spectators and the ringmaster came out and greeted us with a booming "Ladies and gentlemen, children of all ages: Welcome to the circus." It was all very exciting and we could hardly wait for the show to begin. The man announced that the first act, directly from Africa, was a quartet of trained elephants. We were just about busting when Naomi, Shirley, Alma, and Zelda lumbered out, decked in bright red harnesses with little plumes of feathers in bonnets on top of their heads. They looked beautiful and were obviously excited to show their tricks. Our friend, the elephant man, was dressed in a bright red suit and as he gave commands, the girls did their tricks while the calliope played circus music. We could hardly contain ourselves! Our elephant friends doing such marvelous stunts! Just as they finished an act where they all stood on top of big round platforms and twirled around, Dewey yelled, "Good girl, Zelda! Way to go." Zelda turned and started to walk toward us. She had recognized Dewey's voice.

"Dewey, shut up! You'll get us in trouble," I raged. But when Zelda saw us, the other elephants also looked our way and suddenly the whole group moved toward us and stuck their trunks in our hands.

"Oh, no! Now we're in for it," Dougie assumed.

"Back, Zelda; Back, Alma; Back, Shirley; Back, Naomi!" the elephant man commanded. The elephants obeyed and he whispered something to them. Then he turned and said to the audience, "Sorry, folks. Those boys have been helping me with the elephants--washing, feeding, and exercising them. That is why the animals responded to them." All eyes turned to us. We about busted with pride. We were now the most important thirteen-year-old boys in town, if not the county. We were elephant boys.

The show continued with high-wire walkers, jugglers, and lions, and so much fun stuff that we could hardly contain ourselves. The clowns had a funny act that ended with them chasing each other with a bucket of water, finally throwing it into the crowd. Luckily the water turned out to be confetti. We were in the perfect position to get covered with the stuff, much to our delight. What a day!

When the show was over, we ambled back through the crowded midway and many people stopped to talk to us about being elephant boys. We loved the attention. Even the east-side guys passed by and congratulated us on our good fortune.

Finally we went by the elephants. They squealed and swept over us with their trunks.

"The elephants really like you guys," the elephant man grinned.

"We like them, too," Dougie echoed. "Sorry that we interfered with your show."

"Oh, that was nothing! Don't worry about it," he reassured us.

It was time for their walk, so we each took our special elephant to the vacant lot. The elephants held our hands, followed us, and we commanded them with "Hup" and "Back" just to prove to our friends that we really were elephant boys. Soon a crowd had gathered. Then it was time to return them to their pens for feeding and watering.

We were walking mighty tall when we went back to the midway. "How much money do you have?" I inquired.

"I've got two dollars and fifty cents," Dougie said.

"Two dollars and a quarter," Chick said.

"I've got eighty-five cents," Dewey reported.

"I've got a dollar and ninety cents," I said. "That's enough for four tickets to the evening show--or we could eat it all up."

"Show," said Dougie.

"Yup, show," said Chick.

"Well, there will be enough money left for popcorn and stuff, so I vote show, too," Dewey chimed in.

Good! That was settled. We bought tickets for the second show and then proceeded to buy as much food as we could with the money left over.

When the second show was over, we were stuffed with junk food and just about worn out from clapping and laughing so hard. We strolled down the midway, soaking up the final moments of circus bliss. "Wow, this has been the best day we ever had," Dewey said.

"Yeah! No foolin'," sighed Dougie.

The circus was shutting down so we got our bikes and rode past the elephant pen and said good night to our friends and then rode home, exhausted.

The next morning we gathered at Dougie's and picked a few tomatoes and cucumbers from his mom's garden to take to the elephants. When back at the circus grounds, we couldn't believe our eyes. Almost everything was down and loaded on the trucks. There were a few men carrying the last boxes and things so we walked to the elephant truck. The girls spotted us through the bars on the windows and began to squeal when they saw us. "Come to say goodbye?" asked the elephant man.

"Yeah! We didn't think you'd be going so soon," I lamented. "Gotta move on! We have a show tomorrow night in Iowa, so it's time to hit the road," he replied.

"We brought the girls a snack. Okay if we feed them?" "Sure! Go ahead," he said with a smile. We crawled up and fed these last treats to our friends; then we patted them on their heads and said goodbye. They rubbed us with their trunks and it seemed that they were sad to leave us.

"You made friends with them," the man said. "They usually don't like strangers. Thanks for the help and kindness to the girls."

We swallowed hard, and blinked a little, but we managed to say that we had had a stupendous time; that his elephants were special to us and we thanked him for allowing us to make friends with them. Soon the trucks were pulling out, leaving big clouds of dust behind. The elephants squealed as they pulled away; we waved.

We watched until they were out of sight.

"Well," Dougie sighed, "what should we do now?"

"I'm ready for a swim," I said.

"Yeah! Me, too," replied Chick.

"Let's go! Last one in is a booger," Dewey said, as he jumped on his bike and headed for the Gosey.

The circus was an experience that we would relive for years. We would reminisce while sitting by a campfire, or when lying under the stars on a summer night, about the moments we spent with the great, gray beasts that were as gentle and loving as kittens. We would never forget Naomi, Shirley, Alma, and Zelda and the days when we were the elephant boys.

Dog Days

The four of us were lounging in the water at the Gosey. It was hot. It was so hot that we were hardly able to leave the water to swing on our tree rope.

"I'm getting cooked in this water," Dewey said.

"Yeah. It's like a bathtub," Chick said.

"I know, but what can we do about it?" I asked.

"These are the dog days of summer," Chick said. "My mom mentioned it this morning."

"I know what it feels like to be boiled like a hot dog," Dewey said. We all laughed at Dewey.

"The river would be cooler because there is a current," Dougie said.

"Yeah, but our moms will kill us if we swim in the river," I said.

"How they gonna know?" Chick said.

"My mom says there are whirlpools that will suck you down, and deep drop-offs you could fall from, never to come up again," Dewey said.

"Dewey, how many times has your mom been swimming in the river?" Dougie asked.

"Well, I don't know, but she said it's dangerous, so... well, I ... "

"Right, just as I said, she probably hasn't ever been in the river; any of our moms, for that matter, so how do they know?"

Dougie had a good point. "Do you ever remember anybody drowning in the river?" he questioned. We thought about that, but we couldn't come up with anyone except the French guy who drowned in the Gosey a long time ago.

"Yeah, how do our moms know?" Chick said.

It didn't take too much talking for us to decide to wade to the end of the Gosey where it met the river. When we arrived, we could see the swirling current, but we stepped in.

"Wow! This is cool and comfortable," remarked Dougie. "Yeah! Much better than back there," I said. We swam a short distance in the river to a sandbar. We found a decent-sized drop-off and soon we were screaming, running, and jumping into the deep water, having a ball. We played on the sandbar all afternoon and then waded back, got our clothes, and headed home.

We stopped at Dougie's house.

"Let's go back tomorrow with our fishing poles," suggested Dougie.

"Yeah! Let's! Then we can swim and fish," Dewey said. Chick thought it sounded like a good plan so we agreed to meet at Dougie's the next morning for a day of fishing and swimming. I asked my mom to make me a lunch to take fishing. I met the guys at Dougie's house. We had our poles, lunches, and canteens of water for our day at the river.

We rode to the Gosey, stripped down, waded into the river, and swam to the sandbar with our lunches and fishing poles held high over our heads. Once on the sandbar, we fooled around for a while and then we decided to get serious about fishing. Dougie had his jackknife with him so he swam to the closest wooded area and cut four pole holders for each of us. We put worms on our hooks and cast into the deep water below the sandbar. We sat in the sand, waiting for a bite.

"It is cool to fish here. Maybe we will catch real fish; not those useless little bluegills we usually end up with," Chick remarked.

"Yeah! A real monster! A big catfish would be great," Dewey

said. It was true. There were rumors of catfish, the size of a small boy, in the river and we all hoped to tangle with one someday.

Soon Dougie had a bite that turned out to be a walleye.

"Wow! We don't find these in the river bottoms," he said. He put the fish on a stringer and put it in the water. A few minutes later Chick caught a catfish and I caught a small-mouth bass.

"Jeepers! This is much better than fishing in the Gosey," I said. Just then Dewey got a bite, set his hook, and watched his pole bend over. He got to his feet and backed onto the sandbar just as a huge fish stripped offline from his reel. "It's one of those monster catfish," he yelled as he fought the fish. We reeled up our poles and gave him space to battle his fish. He managed to bring the fish close to the sandbar where it came to the surface of the water. When we realized it was a huge gar, about three feet long, with a mouthful of sharp teeth and an evil look on its face, we took a step backward.

"Unbelievable! Dewey, it's a big gar," Dougie said. "Somebody grab him and take the hook out," Dewey said. "Yeah, right! Have you seen those teeth, Dewey?" objected Chick.

"C'mon guys, take him off for me," begged Dewey.

"No way, Dewey. You caught him. You take him off," instructed Dougie.

Dewey dragged the fish to the shore and walked over warily to inspect it. "Jeez, it's ugly. It looks like a crocodile," he said. He handled the fish with care in order to position the hook between his fingers and then he attempted to remove it from the jaw of the fish. Just as he did, the fish began to thrash and snap its jaws. Dewey dropped it and ran for cover. "You better be careful, Dewey. You'll loose your weenie," Chick said. We all laughed at that, except Dewey.

"You guys are a lot of help. I'm gonna cut the line and give him the hook," he announced. We thought that was a good idea so Dougie gave Dewey his knife. He released the fish and pushed it into the water with his foot. The gar delayed for a minute.

Then, little by little, it swam off into the deep water.

"Whooie! I hate to think of swimming here with those big things," Dougie said. "One might come along and make you a sit-down pee'er." We thought that was hilarious and laughed at Dougie's joke.

We ate our lunch under a hot sun. "Wow! I'm cookin'!" Dougie said. "I'm gonna sit in the water and fish." That was a super suggestion so we sat down and the water came up to our necks. We held our poles in one hand and watched for bites.

"This is great," Chick said. It was cool looking, too: four heads, and four hands holding fishing poles, sticking out of the water. Soon we were catching catfish and bass and walleyes, and the day slipped by. When we caught a fish, we crawled to our stringer, attached the fish, and returned to our sitting position in the water. By late afternoon, all the stringers were nicely filled with fish and we decided to call it quits. We waded back to our clothes and bikes.

"Now, don't tell anyone we were in the river," Dougie said.

"Then we can return without getting into trouble." We agreed to keep this place a secret. Off we went to our homes to clean our fish and have supper. As I worked on my fish in the backyard, my mom strolled up to check out my catch.

"Where did you get those?" she asked. "What?"

"The bass, catfish, and walleyes," she said.

"Uh, down at the, by Gutweiler's stream," I stammered.

"Gutweiler's stream? Where is that?"

"Well, it's where the water in Gutweiler's Lake comes out. It's like a little river," I said.

"Since when does Gutweiler's Lake, or its stream, have catfish, walleyes, and smallmouth bass?"

My mouth was hanging open like I was a simpleton. First of all, how did mom know what a catfish or a walleye or a smallmouth was in the first place; and secondly, how did she know they weren't in Gutweiler's Lake?

"Well, I'm waiting for an answer." I didn't have one.

"Have you been at the river?" She knew without me answering so there was no point in telling a lie.

"Yeah, we went to the river because the Gosey was too hot."

"The Gosey? You've been in the Gosey, too?" She must be in the FBI! Where was she getting all this information? "I thought you were fishing in the sloughs."

"You know where the Gosey is?" I asked.

"Of course, I do. Do you think I've never been near the river?" Yeah. That was exactly what I thought.

"Your dad and I used to fish at the river before we had you kids."

"Fish? You fished?"

"Of course, and I'm a pretty darn good fisherman, too."

You could have knocked me over with a puff of wind. My mom was a fisherman!

"Do the other mothers know you guys hang around the river?"

"Oh c'mon, Mom. Don't tell. They'll kill me for getting caught."

"Okay, I won't tell. But, you boys be careful and stay out of the water. Just fish; don't swim."

I nodded my head; somehow thinking I was agreeing with the fishing part and ignoring the swimming part. "Okay, we'll be careful. Wouldn't want to fall into any whirlpools or something," I grinned.

"You won't think it's funny if you fall in and drown," she said. When I finished cleaning the fish, I called Dougie and told him what had happened. "My dad saw my fish and he knew I didn't get them in the bottoms," he said. Well, I didn't feel so badly after all. Dougie also got caught. Chick phoned later to say he got busted, too. Then, after supper, Dewey called and said he had gotten the third degree from his dad and had also spilled the beans. We all were discovered. Who would have thought that adults knew one fish from another? Fortunately our parents did not forbid us to go to the river but we were each told to be safe and to stay out of the water. Well, it was too late so, until we got caught, we planned to stay quiet.

It was amusing that our parents were so educated on the kinds of fish. We never imagined they knew anything about fish. You'd have thought they were once young, and learned what we knew, and somehow never forgot. Maybe they recalled all the fun times they had enjoyed at the river so they allowed us to go. Who knows? From then on, we had a greater respect for their knowledge of the outdoors. We enjoyed swimming in the river hundreds of times that summer, and for that matter, for many summers following. And, surprisingly, we never once saw one of those deadly whirlpools.

Take Me Out to the Ball Game

Chick, Dewey, and I were sitting in my backyard, waiting for Dougie and the rest of the guys to come over for a game of baseball. We had practice a couple days each week and we usually played a game with the east-side boys once or twice a week on the off days.

Dougie was riding in as fast as his bike would carry him and he slid to a screeching halt, throwing up a cloud of dust from the alley.

"Hey, guys! You wanna go to a Braves game?" "Braves? Milwaukee Braves?" I exclaimed. "Yeah, The Milwaukee Braves!"

"How? When?" We were on our feet asking Dougie questions all at once.

"One of the teachers at my school organized this trip. He calls it "The Knot-Hole Club." It costs two dollars for the game and a dollar for the bus ride. It's a great deal," Dougie reported.

"But, it's through the public school," Dewey cautioned. "We can't go. We go to St. John's."

"That doesn't matter. It's for any kid in town," Dougie reassured.

"No foolin'? Dougie, you wouldn't fool us," Chick said.

"No foolin'! Look! Here is the form your parents can sign to give their permission for you to go," he said, as he pulled folded, crumpled forms from his pocket. We each took one of the wrinkled sheets and read it over. It was true! The following week, a bus trip to attend a Braves game!! We wanted to jump up and down.

We had to come up with three dollars, get our parents' permission, and return the form to the school. We raced home to start in on our parents. Practice was cancelled for the day.

"I'll give you money for the game and bus ride and an extra two dollars," Mom said after I explained this great opportunity to her. I couldn't believe my ears. I expected an uphill battle in persuading her to let me go and then a ton of pestering for the money part of it. The surprise was written all over my face.

"What? Didn't you think I'd agree?" she asked.

"I just didn't expect you to say yes so quickly," I confessed. She smiled, signed the form, and handed over three dollars.

"Sometimes moms and dads are human, too," she reminded me. I decided there and then that she was a pretty darn good mom.

I raced to Dougie's house on my bike and found that he had his form signed, too. Soon Chick and Dewey arrived with the required signature and we headed for the school office. It was the first time I had ever been in the public school and, actually, it was quite nice. I expected it to be like a prison or something because that was the idea we got when the sisters talked about it. Somehow it didn't seem to be a terrible place after all. The teacher, who had organized the trip, was helpful and seemed delighted that Dougie had invited us. Dougie was proud of himself, too.

Well, for the next week, we were on a high! The trip was all we talked about, and no matter what we were doing-baseball, swimming or fishing-the conversation always came back to the upcoming trip.

The morning of the trip arrived and we assembled at the bus garage an hour before departure. Every kid in town was there and we could hardly wait for the bus door to open. Everyone was wearing a baseball cap and most of us were extra prepared by carrying our baseball gloves-in the event a ball should come our way. We were like a bunch of chattering monkeys, all trying to get on the bus at the same time. The teacher called our names, we yelled here, and climbed on. Our four names were called first so we got to sit in the choice seats in the back of the bus. The rest of our team and the east-side guys were also aboard, as well as many kids from the public school. It was fantastic.

The bus pulled out of town and the noise was almost deafening. Everyone was chattering at the same time. If the energy in that bus could have been harnessed, the city could have been lit for a week. After an hour, things quieted down and someone started singing A Hundred Bottles if Beer on the Wall Everyone joined in and sang until we got down to one bottle if beer. The bus driver and the adults must have been relieved when the song was over. To this day, I can't figure out why the bottles of beer were "on" the wall. Why weren't they in the refrigerator? Oh, well. It was a fun song.

The miles swept by and we were nearing Milwaukee County Stadium, the home of the Milwaukee Braves. We became super excited and the noise level went through the roof again. The teacher had planned it so we would arrive at the stadium in time to watch batting practice. Of course, we planned on catching a fly ball and getting it autographed. We figured the Braves surely knew we were coming and players would be waiting for us, eager to give their autographs.

The scenery had changed from trees and grass to buildings as we approached the big city. The buildings were of greater dimensions than anything at home, for sure. At home, the hotel, at three stories, was the tallest building. In Milwaukee, there were massive structures, stretching up twenty or thirty stories. We were very impressed. Then we came to the freeway exit to the stadium. There it was: Milwaukee County Stadium. It was like Mecca or the Vatican. It was the home of the Braves. How many times had we listened to games being broadcast on the radio from this place? How many legendary baseball heroes had stood at home plate, tapping the dirt from their spikes? It was like a religious experience. We couldn't wait to get off the bus and get inside.

We stood in line and handed our tickets to a man in a blue uniform. He tore them in half, giving us a torn half back. We went through a turnstile thing and then up the stairs to the field. We were running through a tunnel toward the sunlight and suddenly we emerged in-Milwaukee County Stadium. We stopped and drank in the moment. The field was amazing. The grass was green-green and it had been mowed back and forth in a manner that gave it diamond patterns. The infield was as smooth as brown silk and chalked with lines running to the bases. The stadium towered above us with row upon row of green seats. There were thousands of them. Pennants flew from the upper deck railing and the scoreboard was lit up like a Christmas tree. It was totally amazing to us.

"Wow! This place is huge," Dougie marveled. "And look at all the seats," Chick said, gapingly. "Look! A hot-dog guy," Dewey said.

"Dewey, only you would think of your stomach at a time like this," I teased. We all laughed at Dewey.

"Hey, hot-dog guy!" Dewey said, breaking the effect of the moment.

"Dewey, don't you ever get full?" Chick asked.

"It's been a long time since breakfast," Dewey said as he waved at the guy who came over and Dewey bought a hot dog. They smelled pretty good so we each bought one, too.

"See, I knew you guys were hungry," Dewey said, licking the mustard off his lip.

We were hanging over the railing in the right-field bleachers when several Braves team members ran to the field to take batting practice. There they were, for real; the guys we listened to on the radio; the ones we read about in the newspaper; the guys whose baseball cards we collected. They were our heroes: Eddie Mathews, Johnny Logan, and Joe Adcock. Soon outfielders appeared and began to catch fly balls. "Hey, there's Hammerin' Hank," Dougie said, pointing to Henry Aaron. Henry was only in his second year at Milwaukee and he was a great hitter.

"I bet he'll hit a homer today," Chick said.

"Yeah, he might," I said. "He's a pretty good long-ball hitter." "Hey, Hank!" Dewey yelled. Hank turned, smiled, and waved.

"Wow! That was cool," Dewey said. We were leaning on the railing, watching, and soon a long ball was coming straight at us. Hammerin' Hank shot over and caught it at the wall below us.

"Nice catch, Hank," Dougie cheered. "Hi, guys," Hank replied. "Hi, Hank," we yelled in unison.

"I see you guys have your baseball gloves. Do you play a lot?"

Henry Aaron was actually talking with us!

"Uh, yeah! We play almost every day," Dougie stammered. "Yeah! We got our own field and everything," Chick added. "We're all big Braves fans," I said.

"That's great! Enjoy the game," Hank said, and he trotted off to center field.

"That was the coolest!" Dewey murmured.

"Yeah, no foolin'! Hank's a good guy. I hope he makes it in the big leagues," I said.

"Me, too. If he always hits like he does now, he'll turn into a great player," Chick said. We all wanted Hank to make it big.

The stands were filling up so we picked our seats in the bleachers and got ready for the game. We were wearing our ball gloves in case a homer came our way so we'd be ready. Vendors were coming by with hot dogs, peanuts, ice cream bars, popcorn, and soda, so we were kept busy eating almost everything that passed by.

Finally the game began and the Braves took the field first. Warren Spahn was pitching. He was one of our favorites so we yelled and cheered at every pitch. It was a good game. After the seventh-inning stretch, we sang Take Me Out to the Ballgame with the announcer. When the Braves came up to bat in the eighth, Hank was up, and on the third pitch he blasted a long ball toward us. We were yelling and had our gloves in the air to catch the ball. On it came. It cleared the railing and hit the bleachers about ten rows below us. It bounced into the air and was coming our way when a guy, sitting two rows down, jumped up and caught it in his bare hands. We just sat there with our mouths open in disbelief: how close we had come to catching a stadium ball!

"Crap! That guy intercepted our ball," Dougie pouted.

"We should pound knots on his head," Chick said.

"I dropped my pop when I stood up to catch it," Dewey said. "Hey, Mister! That ball was coming to us," I said. He turned around and smiled but he didn't offer to give us the ball. We were very disappointed. If Hank ever turned out to be a famous player, we would have had a notable trophy.

All too soon, the game was over. The Braves won and we were as delighted as a bunch of boys could be. We made our way out of the stadium and back to the bus. When a head count was taken, every body was accounted for so we were able to take off for home. The bus was packed with excited kids carrying home souvenirs. Some had pennants; others had ball caps, or Braves jerseys. None of us had money for anything expensive so we cherished our programs and the memories of almost catching a home run ball and talking to Henry Aaron. It didn't take long for A Hundred Bottles of Beer ... to start again and by the time we got to the twentieth bottle of beer we were in Madison. The driver took us to a new restaurant called McDonald's. Supposedly we could buy fifteen-cent hamburgers and ten-cent French fries. We piled out of the bus and went in. Instead of sitting and waiting for a waitress, we walked up to a counter and gave our order to an employee behind the counter. The food was ready and came down slides from the kitchen. The employee picked up the order and stuffed it in a sack. We each had enough money to order three hamburgers, two fries, and a chocolate shake, so we handed the guy a dollar and got a dime back! It was such a good deal that we decided to buy another bag of fries. Back to the bus we went, with our bags of food. "This is cool," Dewey said. "You get a lot of stuff for a dollar."

"No foolin'! This is a good place," Dougie chimed in.

"I hope they stay in business. How can they sell food so cheaply and make money?" Chick wondered.

"Enjoy it while we can. It won't be around long," I said.

The bus quieted because we were involved with our meals and then many of the kids slid down in their seats and dozed off I t was getting dark and we had all gotten up early so everyone was tired. The next thing we knew the bus was pulling into the public school parking lot and the bus lights came on. "Time to wake up, sleepy heads," our chaperone announced. We yawned and groaned and made our way to the front of the bus. "Thanks for the swell trip," we all said.

"You're welcome. I hope you had a wonderful time."

"It was the best ever," we said.

We got our bikes and said goodbye to each other and made plans for a ball game the next day. "Let's start at two o'clock," Dougie said. "I think I'll sleep till at least noon." No fooling! That sounded good.

As tired as I was, it was difficult to sleep. Every time I closed my eyes, I could see Milwaukee County Stadium. I could see the grass, the seats, and I heard the crowd cheering. I could smell the hotdogs and popcorn. From now on, when we listened to ball games on the radio, it would be different. We could close our eyes and see it happening. And I thought about Henry Aaron. Gosh, I hoped he would make it in the big leagues. It would be impressive to tell people that I had talked to him once.

The Menagerie

Dougie and I were critter collectors. We loved animals and we each had a private zoo in our backyard. Dougie's critter house had once been a woodshed. It had an outside chicken-wire pen with partitions and it made a great home for his pets. His pride and joy was his rabbit, Zsa Zsa. She was a beautiful, white rabbit; she was tame and loved to be petted. Dougie also had homing pigeons as well as regular pigeons. There was an older kid in town that raised homers so we each had bought a pair of them from him. Dougie also had his dog, Cookie, who was good at his one trick of sitting up and begging for food; a trick, but nothing spectacular.

My dog, Butch, had been rescued by my dad from the dog pound. He was a friendly guy so my dad felt sorry for him and brought him home. Butch was fairly old when he came to live with us so he didn't know cool tricks. He liked to play ball and sleep; mainly he slept. He was a great friend.

My zoo consisted of a collection of little sheds that I had built myself About a year earlier, before Dougie had moved to town, I had been at Walsh's grocery store and was checking out the live chickens in the storage yard. They had a shed for the chickens that the farmers sold or traded for food, while they waited for the butcher to prepare them for sale in the store. I always liked to look for eggs in the pens. Eggs came in handy for one thing or another, especially if we were having a war with the east-side guys. One day I went to Walsh's and I saw strange looking chickens in the pens. They were small and pretty. Instead of being plain white, they were shades of red, black, and gold. I had never seen chickens like that, so I went in and asked the butcher about them. "Those are bantams, or ban ties, for short," he said.

"Why are they so puny?" I asked.

"That's their size. They lay small eggs, too," he said. Hmm, they were cute, so I asked him for a price and he quoted me a quarter apiece. What a bargain! I paid up and asked if I could leave them there until I got a chicken house built.

My neighbor, Fred, had a pile of used lumber behind his garage and I asked him if! could borrow some of it. He gave me the go-ahead. He suggested that I attach my chicken house to the side of his garage that bordered our backyard. That way I'd only have to build three walls and the pen would be extra sturdy. Fred was a smart guy and a good neighbor.

I began work on my chicken house and I completed it in a few days. It looked like a long outhouse, about six feet tall and ten feet long. I used chicken wire to make a pen on the front. Then I cut a little door in the wall and made small boxes for nests and set a few poles for the chickens to roost on. Fred gave it the inspection and said I had done a good job.

I went to the feed mill for a bag of chopped-up corncobs for the floor. Then I went to Walsh's and picked up my chickens. There were three hens and one rooster. I took them home, turned them loose in the pen, and they seemed to like it real well. I guess anything was nicer than the shed at Walsh's and getting your head lopped off. They looked around, then went inside to check out their new home. They were pretty cool chickens and the next morning I found a little egg in one of the boxes. The rooster crowed every morning.

It didn't take long until I had collected a few more hens and then I let one of them sit on a batch of eggs and soon I had about a dozen banty chickens. Then I met Dougie and saw his pigeons, so I decided to raise pigeons, too. That meant an addition to my chicken house and another outside pen, so-back to Fred's for more lumber. After the pigeon business, I decided I wanted a rabbit. I bought a black one from a kid in town and I named her Snowball. After that, I got a free squirrel from a kid that had raised two of them. My zoo was growing.

One day I was riding my bike past the salvage yard on the outside of town and I spotted a large tub on the ground. It looked like it would be the perfect thing for making a turtle farm. The man who owned it said I could have it. I went back, taking Dougie with me, and we rolled the tub to my house. We filled it halfway with sand and buried an old dish pan in the sand. Then we put water in the dish pan. Now we needed turtles, so we went to Gutweiler's Lake and fished until we caught a couple and then took them to their new home. We caught insects and dug worms for them. After that, whenever we caught a turtle while we were fishing, we added it to the turtle exhibit. I had a great zoo!

There was a partially burned factory on the edge of town that was home to lots of pigeons. We decided to go there after dark when the pigeons were sleeping and catch a few for our pigeon collections. Dewey and Chick wanted to help so one night we rode our bikes to the old factory. Dewey didn't have a place for a zoo and his mom wouldn't let him have anything except a little turtle in a plastic dish with a little plastic palm tree in it. Chick's mom had a cat and wouldn't let him add other critters to his backyard so they both enjoyed coming with us, helping us develop our zoos.

"This place is creepy," Dewey said, as we went through a creaky door.

"Shhh! Dewey. Don't talk so loudly. You'll wake up the pigeons," Dougie instructed.

110

We walked upstairs to the second floor and shined our flashlights toward the ceiling, expecting to see a ton of pigeons. There weren't any to be seen.

"Where are the pigeons?" I whispered.

"Hey, look," Chick said, pointing his light toward a trap door in the ceiling. "I'll bet this is the attic."

"The pigeons are probably up there," Dougie said. We shined our lights around and located an old desk and a few wooden crates which we stacked below the attic opening.

"I'll go up and take a look," said Chick.

He crawled up and stuck his head into the attic. Soon he lifted himself up and disappeared into the black hole. We all stood there, staring up, and suddenly Chick's face appeared out of the blackness, "Millions of pigeons up here."

"No foolin'?" Dougie remarked.

"They're sitting on beams all over the place."

The three of us climbed up and turned on our flashlights to reveal pigeons-everywhere!

"Guess we've got all the pigeons we'd ever want," exclaimed Dougie.

"Let's try to catch a few real pretty ones," I said. "Spread out and try not to spook them."

We crept through the rafters and the pigeons began cooing and fluttering around.

"They're getting nervous," Chick said.

"Let's try to each catch two and then we can come back later and take a few more," I suggested.

Just then I spotted a rare white one and I reached up to get it. As my hand touched the pigeon, it took off. When that pigeon flew, so did the rest of them. There were pigeons taking off and flying everywhere and the quiet turned into chaos. The beating of the pigeon's wings made a lot of wind, like a hurricane. Soon there were pigeon feathers, pigeon poop, and dust everywhere.

''Jeepers! They're attacking," Dewey hollered. "Just grab a couple, Dewey," Dougie shouted.

Chick and I each had two pigeons. Dougie had a pretty one and was trying to catch another. Dewey was still attempting to make his first capture. A nice one landed above him and he reached up and caught it.

"Hey! I got one!" he boasted, as he turned to show me. He took one step forward and suddenly there was a huge crashing sound and Dewey disappeared. One second, I was looking at Dewey; the next second, he was gone. I shined my light where he had been and I saw a big hole in the floor--which was actually the ceiling of the room below. I peered down and there was Dewey, on his back.

"Dewey, are you okay?"

"Yeah! I still have my pigeon, too," he said, holding it up for us to see.

"Let's get out of here," Chick said. "These pigeons are riled up. We can come back another night."

It sounded like a good idea. I took one of Dougie's pigeons and Chick took the other and he climbed down. Then we passed the pigeons down to him and he put them in the little cage we had brought. Chick and I climbed down. Dewey was still sitting on the floor petting his pigeon. "He's a nice one, huh?"

"Yeah, Dewey. He's a beauty." We put Dewey's pigeon in the cage and made our way outside.

"Whew, that was fun!" Dewey declared.

"Gosh, Dewey, I thought you'd be complaining about falling through the ceiling," Chick responded.

"I got a pigeon, though," Dewey said. Dewey was mighty proud of his pigeon. Of course, he didn't have a place to keep his pigeon so he decided to keep it at my house.

"I think I'll name it Frank," he said.

Since Dougie and I were the only ones with pigeon pens, we inherited all the pigeons. It appeared that they liked their new homes and we took good care of them, feeding them well. We made more raids on the old factory until the pigeons caught on to what we were doing and they became so nervous when we showed up that they would fly around, making a terrible mess, so we left them be. We had plenty of pigeons, anyway.

One day, when Dougie and I were by Walsh's storage shed, we saw a pigeon fly into a hole in the eaves. "Hey, did you see that?" Dougie asked.

"Yeah, let's see if we can catch him," I said. We parked our bikes and looked up at the hole in the eave. You could see the pigeon sitting inside looking out at us. "See that pipe on the side of the building?" I asked. "One of us could shinny up that pipe, reach around the side of the eave, and grab the pigeon."

"I'll do it," Dougie offered. "You be ready to take him in case there are others inside."

The pipe coming through the wall was attached to a rod that came up from the bottom of the building. Dougie began to climb it. When he was halfway up, the pipe detached from the rod at the bottom and came crashing to the ground. When it hit, the end broke off and black stuff came gushing out, covering me.

Dougie had fallen off the pipe when it hit the ground and he rolled into the black stuff.

"What the heck is it?" Dougie asked because he was covered.

He stuck his finger into the substance and smelled it.

"It smells sweet, like pancake syrup."

I sniffed it and tasted it. "It does. What should we do with this broken pipe?" I inquired.

"I don't know, but I think we best get out of here," Dougie insisted, and we hopped on our bikes and beat it toward his house.

"We can't go to my house covered in this stuff," Dougie blurted. "Let's wash it off at the Gosey," he suggested. We removed our syrup-soaked clothes, waded into the water, and scrubbed the sticky stuff off. It came out easily enough and then we hung the clothes in the trees to dry. Meanwhile, we took a nice swim and then we relaxed in the shallow water. "I wonder how much of that stuff squirted out of the pipe?" I mused.

"Probably, not much. Someone likely noticed and turned it off at the source," he said. At least, that was what we hoped.

An hour or so later our clothes were dry so we dressed and rode our bikes to Dougie's house. We were in his pigeon pen when his dad came into the yard. "You guys been at Walsh's today?"

"Why?"

"Someone broke their sorghum pipe and about a hundred gallons of the stuff poured out on the ground," relayed Dougie's father.

"Sorghum? What's sorghum?" His dad looked at us; then walked over to Dougie and pointed at his tennis shoe.

"That's sorghum! The black stuff all over your shoes!" he scolded.

Busted!

We knew better than to try to lie our way out of this one so we admitted that we had broken the pipe but that it had been one huge accident.

"And, just what were you doing on that pipe?" he wanted to know.

"We saw a pigeon and tried to catch it," Dougie said.

"Pigeon? How many pigeons do you have?" We had no idea. "How did they know we did it?" I finally asked.

"A worker saw you riding past the store, drenched in sorghum. Didn't take a genius to figure that one out," he added.

"Well, I must head to the store to pay for the sorghum that you two Einsteins spilled. Stay here until I get back."

Dougie's dad was gone for about fifteen minutes but it seemed like fifteen hours. When he returned, he looked peeved. "Well, your little pigeon raid cost me forty-seven dollars," he said. Forty-seven dollars! We wouldn't see an allowance again until college! Dougie's dad must have realized how badly we felt. "I know you guys weren't trying to break it, and that it was an accident. I'll pay for it but you two stay out of trouble for the rest of the summer." We couldn't believe our ears!

"Thanks, Dad!" Dougie said, and he hugged his father. "Yeah, thanks," I said. Then I hugged him, too. He grinned and told us to go take care of our zoos.

"Wow! Your dad is a cool guy," I said.

"Yeah! No kidding. I thought we were dead," Dougie stated, very relieved.

"Let's see what the other guys are doing," I said.

We hopped on our bikes and rode to Chick's house, then to Dewey's. The four of us rode to the river for a couple of hours of fishing. We were sitting side by side on the riverbank fishing. "You know," Dougie said to me, "a long time from now, when we have our own kids, maybe we'll think back to this and give them a break if they do something stupid." Yeah, that sounded fair, but at that time, we didn't even LIKE girls, so that would be a long time off!

A Found Lure

If you ever look my way and don't see me, come over, and you'll find a puddle," Dewey whined from right field.

"Yeah! It's so hot, my glove won't stay on my sweaty hand," Dougie said.

It was hot. It was probably the hottest day of the summer, and we were playing ball with the east-side guys. It was just past noon and the sun was beating down, turning our outfield into the Sahara Desert. Sweat was trickling into our eyes and our shirts were soaked and sticking to our backs.

"Hey, let's call the game, and go for a swim!" Johnny Deagan said. Everyone agreed that it was way too hot to play ball, so we picked up the bases, put them in my neighbor Fred's garage, hopped on our bikes, and headed for the Gosey.

Usually we kept the Gosey to ourselves, but today the east-side guys were joining us. Both teams were short a few players, so instead of a group of eighteen kids, there were about a dozen of us. Some kids were on vacation and some had stayed home because of the heat.

Johnny Deagan was the leader of the east-side guys. He was going to be in ninth grade in the fall, so he was the oldest and probably the coolest. He was tall and good-looking, and instead of being skinny like the rest of us, he had muscles. His clothes were clean and nicely fit. His hair was always perfect, and he stood out as someone you wanted to have as a friend. The girls followed him around like a litter of puppies and he even LIKED girls. Most of us were still repulsed by girls and their silly, giggly ways. Johnny always told us that some day we'd change our minds. Right now it was too hot to think about anything but getting our clothes off and getting into the water.

We threw up a massive cloud of dust as we sped down the dirt road to the Gosey. When we arrived, we parked our bikes, stripped, and jumped into the cool water. It didn't take long for the quiet pool to turn into a wild, thrashing cauldron of screaming boys, dunking each other, and having a great time.

Our rope swing was mounted so that it hung out over the Gosey. Long ago, someone had planted a maple tree by an old rock foundation by the riverbank. A thick hay rope was tied to one of its sturdy branches. A hefty knot was tied at the end to support the feet while swinging. We also tied a long string to the end of the rope so we could easily grab the rope when we wanted to swing. Johnny swam to the string and side-armed it to the bank. Then he pulled on the string and the rope and climbed on the tree branch to swing out across the water. "Banzai!" he yelled as he swung out, doing a cannonball into the water, making an impressive splash. We appreciated his stunt and soon we were imitating him, seeing who could make the biggest splash.

It was Johnny's turn again and this time he put his feet on the knot, but when he got to the top of the arc, he held on with his feet and then let go with his hands, did a back flip, and landed in the water, feet first. "Wow, Johnny! That was awesome!" we exclaimed. Johnny was good at everything he did.

Then we played tag. It didn't take long until Chick tagged Dewey and Dewey became IT. Dewey wasn't the fastest swimmer, so when he was IT, we had a lot of fun taunting him, trying to get him to chase us. Johnny was yelling at Dewey, allowing him to get close before ducking underwater and swimming away. Dewey was behind him when he came up for air and he almost tagged him, but Johnny dove again, and swam across the Gosey underwater.

"Hey, Dewey! Over here," Johnny yelled, from the other side of the Gosey.

"No way! I'm not going over there," Dewey said.

"C'mon, Dewey. I'll stay here till you make it over."

Dewey must have had a sudden burst of ambition because he began swimming across the Gosey toward Johnny.

"Here I am, Dewey," Johnny taunted. Dewey was close to him

and Johnny was darting back and forth, waiting for Dewey to commit to one direction or the other.

"Hey, look! A Daredevil," Dewey said, pointing to the lower branch of a tree just behind Johnny.

"I'm not stupid, Dewey. You can't fool me with that old trick."

"No, look. It's hanging in the tree," Dewey said, and he started swimming toward the tree. Johnny took a quick look over his shoulder and then he, too, saw the Daredevil. He spun around and grabbed the lure just before Dewey got to it.

"Hey, that's mine!" Dewey said. "I saw it first."

"Tough, Dewey! I got to it first," Johnny jeered.

"Well, I'm gonna tag you, at least," Dewey said, and he took a quick swipe at Johnny. Of course, Johnny was quicker than Dewey and he dove underwater. He was under for a long period of time when he emerged about halfway across the Gosey, screaming, "Oh, God! Help me! Help me!"

We all laughed as Johnny thrashed around in the water pretending to be in trouble. We figured he was fooling Dewey and would wait for him to get close and then take off swimming again.

"I'm hooked. Help me!" he choked.

Dougie looked at me. "Do you suppose he's really hurt?"

"We better check," I said. Dougie and I swam to Johnny.

When we got there, Johnny was doubled over, barely able to stay afloat.

"What's wrong?" Dougie questioned.

"I got hooked on that Daredevil," Johnny said, through clenched teeth.

By then Dewey had swum over to us and was yelling that he had Johnny and tagged him.

"Where is it?" I said, looking at his hands, thinking he had a hook in his finger.

"It's in my bag," he said.

Dewey, Dougie, and I looked at each other, not understanding what Johnny had meant.

"Your bag? What do you mean?" I asked.

Suddenly, Dewey, Dougie, and I all got it at the same time. Johnny was hooked in his crotch!

"No way!" I said. Johnny nodded his head and rolled on his back. Dougie and I almost fainted.

"Oh, no! Johnny's got the Daredevil hooked in his sack! Dewey shouted.

There, hanging from his most tender part, was the red and white Daredevil!

"Oh man, I'm gonna puke," Dougie said.

"You guys gotta help me to shore. I can't swim," Johnny said, weakly.

Dougie and I each took one of Johnny's arms. He rolled to his back and we towed him to shore. By now all the rest of the guys knew something was really wrong, and when we got to shallow water, they helped us get Johnny to the shore. "Oh, my gosh!" Chick said. "He's got that hook in his bag."

Everyone was grimacing and trying not to look but was fascinated by the lure hanging from Johnny--in a terribly wrong place.

The spoon was about four inches long with a treble hook.

One of the three hooks was through Johnny's scrotum.

"Well, it's good it's there, and not higher," one of the east-side guys said, trying to cheer Johnny up. Johnny just looked at him with a look of murder in his eyes.

"You think it's funny?" he asked.

"No, Johnny. I'm sorry," the kid said.

One guy lived just a few blocks from the Gosey. "Philip, ride home and get a wire cutter so we can cut the barb off the hook," Johnny said. Philip slipped on his shorts, jumped on his bike, and rode off in a cloud of dust. We stood there staring at Johnny who tried to remain very still.

"Does it hurt a lot?" Dewey said.

"Yeah, Dewey. It hurts a lot," Johnny said.

"I'm glad you got that lure now," Dewey said, smiling.

"Dewey, shut up, you idiot! Johnny's in pain," Chick said. Even in his situation, Johnny managed to smile at Dewey.

"It's okay, Dewey. I know you didn't mean any harm. I wish I had let you take the lure, but I wouldn't wish this on anyone." Dewey smiled, and nodded at Johnny.

It seemed like hours until Philip returned. He screeched to a halt, throwing up a huge cloud of dust. He dropped his bike in the sand and came running to the edge of the water where we were surrounding Johnny.

"Here, I couldn't find a wire cutter, so I brought this," he said, holding out a big hunting knife.

"Cripes, get that thing away from me!" Johnny said, rolling on his side to protect his crotch. "You're not gonna cut it out!" Philip looked disappointed, thinking he had done a good thing, and now he was getting yelled at.

"I'll go get a wire cutter," Chick said. "We've got one." He picked up his bike and rode off, and while he was gone, we just stood there, feeling sorry for poor Johnny. A few minutes later, Chick rode back with a huge pair of bolt cutters. "This'll do it," he said, as he ran down the bank to the water's edge. The bolt cutters were bright red with handles about two feet long and with jaws like a piranha's from South America. Johnny looked at the cutter and then at Chick.

"You be careful with that thing. Don't cut anything but the hook," he said, with a nervous laugh. We all laughed, too. We needed something to lighten things up.

"Somebody take hold of the hook and lift it up so I can get at the end of it with the cutter," Chick said.

Everyone looked at everyone else.

"Well, come on. Someone, take hold of it," Johnny ordered.

Nobody wanted to be messing around in that area of a friend's anatomy, but finally Dougie, good, old, cool-headed Dougie, stepped forward and took hold of the hook, and carefully lifted it upward so Chick could remove the barb. Chick put the jaws of the bolt cutter on the hook and pulled the handles together and the hook snapped off like a wet noodle. Then Dougie freed the hook from Johnny's crotch. We were watching open-mouthed as Johnny inspected himself. It seemed that he was in pretty good shape with just a tiny spot of blood. "Looks like I'll live," he said, smiling.

"You better put some iodine on that," Dewey suggested.

We all felt better now. "I think I'll just sit out for a while. You guys go ahead and swim." We waded back into the water but the mood had changed. We swam for a few minutes, then we decided to quit for the day. Johnny slid into his underwear and shorts with a gentle motion and ran his hands through his hair and every hair fell into place. It was perfect again. He tied his T-shirt to his handlebars and put on his shoes and carefully mounted his bike. He was just as cool as ever. The coolest kid in town, tall, tanned, good looking, with a hole in his bag! Anyone that cool, who could handle something like that, deserved our respect.

''Johnny, don't forget this," Dougie said, as Johnny was about to ride off. He tossed the two-hooked Daredevil up the bank to Johnny who caught it and hooked it onto his handlebar.

"Yeah, thanks! After all I went through to get this, it better catch a fish or two for me," he said, laughing.

"It better catch you a world record," I said. Johnny laughed, waved goodbye, and rode off, still the coolest guy in town.

The Pool

It was finally finished. The town had begun construction on a public swimming pool in the early spring and the day of the grand opening arrived. We had been monitoring the progress since the time the hole was dug. We sat on our bikes and watched as they poured concrete into big forms. We looked on as they installed pipes and drains, and then built the changing houses and the office where pool employees would collect money and hand out wire baskets for clothes. When it was finished, they put a fence around the whole complex. It had taken many months to complete the project. Everyone was excited to have a pool in town.

We gathered together as the mayor and other important townsfolk made speeches about the pool and the advantages of having kids swim there instead of in the river. Then they opened the doors and treated everyone to a free swim. We got in line, with about every other kid in town, and received a wire basket with a number on it. We went to the boys' changing room, peeled off our clothes, and put them into the basket. There was a metal safety pin with a number that we removed from the basket and pinned to our swimming suits. The changing room was wall-to-wall boys, all scrambling to get changed and into the pool. Before you could enter the water, you had to pass through a shower room, then through a shallow tank filled with a whitish liquid designed to kill anything that was growing on your feet. Finally, we handed in our baskets at another window and we were ready to swim.

The pool was great. There was a shallow end for the little kids, sectioned off by a rope with plastic floats. The other end was deep and it was equipped with two diving boards. We ran to the diving boards and climbed the ladder to the high board for our first plunge into the pool. "Hey, you guys get back on the other side of the rope!" We turned to see who was being yelled at. The lifeguard was looking at us.

"Who? Us?" Dougie objected.

"Yeah, you! Get back to the little kids' side until you pass your swimming test."

What indignity! We, with the exception of Dewey, could probably swim circles around this guy. He was a college guy hired by the town as head lifeguard. His name was Bob Mick and it seemed that he took his job very seriously.

We walked over to him. "What do we have to do to pass the swimming test?"

"You have to swim the length of the pool and back without stopping." We looked at each other and grinned.

"I'll go first," Dougie volunteered.

"Okay, hotshot. Give it a try," Mr. Mick said.

Dougie walked to the deep end of the pool, dove in, and swam part way underwater, then surfaced and swam the rest of the way doing a crawl. Then he turned at the wall and did the backstroke part of the way back; then side-stroked to the end. "Anything else I can do for you?" he asked, looking up at Mr. Mick.

"Don't be a wise guy," the lifeguard barked. "Who's next?"

"I'll go," said Chick, who copied Dougie's performance. Then Dewey went. He wasn't as graceful as Dougie or Chick but he managed to make it down and back. Then it was my turn, so I dove in and swam the first length with a crawl, turned, swam on my back to the rope, then dove underwater and swam about a foot off the bottom toward the twelve-foot deep end. Underwater, you could hear the sound of the pumps and see the drains that sucked in the water. I stayed on the bottom until I reached the wall, came up the side of the wall like a porpoise, and shot up out of the water. When at the top, I blew a mouthful of water into the air; indeed, a very dramatic move. The water hit Mr. Mick in the face and chest.

"Hey! Watch where you're splashing that water!"

I was hanging onto the side of the pool with a grin on my face and the other guys were laughing at my joke.

"You passed the test, but you have one-half hour out of the pool for splashing."

What? I had just passed my swimming test, but I was being punished. I didn't think I liked this pool very much.

The other guys got in the water and I had to sit on my towel by the fence. It wasn't long until Dewey grabbed Dougie from behind and dunked him. Mr. Mick's whistle made a shrill noise and he pointed at Dewey.

"You! Out for a half hour for dunking!"

Dewey looked around and realized he was the one being corrected this time.

"Who? Me?" he questioned.

"Out of the pool!" The lifeguard was getting spiteful now. Dewey joined me on the concrete and soon the whistle shrieked again and Chick was targeted for running along the side the pool and jumping in. "No running! Out for a half hour," bellowed the lifeguard. Chick joined Dewey and me. Dougie was the only one of our group still in the water. He looked at us, grinned, and then swam to the side of the pool and climbed the ladder to the high diving board. The lifeguard was sitting on a high chair by the diving board, watching the pool. He wore a round hat like you would see in a movie about Africa, hard and shiny. He had wiped off the water I had splashed on him and then he applied tanning lotion. Dougie walked to the end of the diving board and did a can opener into the pool.

A can opener was like a cannon ball, except that the foot was placed against the opposite leg, making a kind of a P-shape. When the diver hit the water, a column of water shot into the air in the direction the P pointed. A cannon ball was just a big splash, but the can opener directed the spray of water.

Well, Dougie did one doozie of a can opener. He hit the water and the splash shot up about fifteen feet and hit the lifeguard in the face, blowing off his African hat. He just about toppled off his chair! He blew his whistle so forcefully that his eyes about popped out of his head. "Out! Out! You're out for the whole day. Get out!" Dougie smiled and picked up his towel. We grabbed our towels and followed him to the changing room.

"You guys, get back here. You haven't put your time in yet."

We stopped. Chick, Dewey, and I looked at each other. Chick nodded and we ran to the deep end of the pool and jumped in. We all did can openers that pointed at the lifeguard. There was such a splash that everything on that end of the pool got wet, including the lifeguard's towel, and his tanning lotion was sent onto the grass under the fence by the wave.

"You guys are all out of here! Get out, now!"

We laughed as we ran toward the changing house. Dougie was waiting for us. We dressed and turned in our empty baskets.

We had been in the new swimming pool for less than a half hour.

"That place is a bummer," Chick grumbled.

"Yeah, all you can do is swim. You can't do anything without getting in trouble," complained Dougie.

"Let's go to the Gosey," I said, and we jumped on our bikes and rode to our old swimming hole. Once there, we stripped off our clothes and piled them on the ground. We didn't need any stupid basket here, or a swimming suit, for that matter. We plunged into the water, splashed and dunked, and did can openers as much as we wanted. And no one blew a dumb whistle at us.

About a week later, we went back to the pool because a free swim day had been organized. In about twenty minutes we were sitting on the concrete, so we gave up and left. We were just not the kind of guys to survive in a pool. There was nothing to do but swim. What fun was that?

Later that week, we were spending the night in a tent, but it was one of those sweltering nights when it never got cool enough to sleep.

"Whew, I'm roasting," Dewey whined.

"No kidding. Let's go swimming," Chick said. We quietly left the tent and wheeled our bikes out of Dougie's backyard until we reached the street. We mounted them and headed toward the river.

"Hey, why don't we try the pool?" Chick suggested.

"How we gonna get in with that barbed wire fence?" I asked. "Well, I noticed the other day that the doors in the changing rooms have locks that can be unlocked from the inside. There is no roof over the changing rooms, so if we boost one guy over the wall, he can go in and unlock the door from the inside." Chick was a criminal genius.

We parked our bikes nearby in a vacant brush-filled lot and gingerly inched our way to the pool area. When we got to the changing house, Dougie and I held our hands together to make a step for Chick. He lifted himself to the top of the wall and grinned as he disappeared over the top. We ran around the corner to the door and heard a click as the door opened. We were giggling like girls as we stripped off our clothes and ran to the pool. Now, this was a treat! You could hear the sound of the water running into the gutters on the sides of the pool as the filter system cycled the water. We jumped in the pool and began having a great time. We played tag and jumped off the diving board and dunked and splashed. The pool was pretty cool without the lifeguard from hell.

We finally decided it was time to return to the tent so we put on our shorts, carried the rest of our clothes, and locked the doors of the changing house. We were cooled off and we smelled like chlorine, but it didn't take long to fall asleep.

A few nights later, when we were sleeping out, we decided to visit the pool again. We proceeded in the same manner and soon we were in the water having great fun. It started to rain but we didn't care because we were wet already. Unexpectedly we heard the lifeguard whistle. We looked up and there was Chick, sitting naked, with the African hat on his head and the whistle around his neck. "You! Out for ten years! Hey, you! Out for the rest of your life!" He was acting big, blowing the whistle, and yelling at us. It was 3 o'clock in the morning.

We were screaming and laughing and making nasty gestures at Chick, having a great time, when Dougie yelled. "Hey, look! The cop!" Sure enough, Mr. Audetta, the town cop, was driving up. We didn't have time to run to the changing house so we huddled in the water against the wall on the side of the pool where he would park. Chick threw the African hat and the whistle on the concrete and jumped into the pool. Mr. Audetta pulled up and shined his lights on the water. We were tight against the side with just our faces out of the water, so he didn't see us. He sat in the car for several minutes with his lights aimed at the pool. Then he drove away. We watched until he was out of sight.

"I bet someone heard Chick playing lifeguard," I said.

"No foolin'! You think so?" Dougie asked.

"That was a close call! Let's get out of here in case he comes back," Dewey said. We dressed and headed on bikes to Chick's house where we were spending the night. As we were settling down, we noticed a car. A spotlight shined on the tent but we stayed motionless. The light went off and Chick peeked out.

"It's him," he said.

"Mr. Audetta?" someone asked in a whisper.

"Yup," replied Chick.

We didn't risk a midnight swim again for a while, giving things time to cool down, but we made it a point to swim in the pool occasionally, and always after hours. The Gosey remained our favorite swimming place. We had a rope swing. Diving was allowed off the big branch. Dunking and splashing were okay. We could scream and make all the noise we wanted and we didn't even have to wear swimming suits. But the best part was no whistle, and no one yelling at us. Later that summer, the town fired Mr. Mick. Parents complained about him being too mean to kids, but we never went back much to swim at the pool, even though he was gone. We had the Gosey, and the only rule there was, "There are no rules."

Gassed

Sleeping out had become a regular thing for Dougie, Dewey, Chick, and me. Dougie and I each had a tent in our backyard that stayed up. After our first disastrous experience with our makeshift "picnic table and refrigerator box" tent, Dougie talked his dad into allowing us to set up their camping tent. We used it repeatedly. My pestering resulted in my parents purchasing a tent for me. I came home from fishing one day and there it was, set up in the backyard. Dewey didn't have a backyard but he was always good for the food detail. His family owned a restaurant and he managed to talk them out of leftovers appropriate for sleep-outs. He would contribute cold French fries or leftover baked potatoes, ham, and chicken. Once he brought prime rib. His mom was pretty mad at him for taking that but we thought it made wonderful sandwiches. Chick had a small tent that was not big enough, so we usually slept in my backyard, or at Dougie's.

Dewey had a gas problem. No matter what he ate, he seemed to end up with gas. It never failed; we would settle in and Dewey would let one go.

"Whoops," he would apologize.

Of course, we would moan and groan and hit Dewey with pillows or tennis shoes and have a great laugh over it. Then we'd settle down again and he'd let another one go.

"Whoops," again.

The rest of us had our days, but Dewey was consistent. He could fart on demand. If we were at a movie, one of us would whisper to Dewey, "Hey, Dewey, let one rip," and he would smile, raise a leg, and let one go. He had one lined up ready for launching just for the asking.

In school, he'd wait until we were working on a group project and then he would rip a loud one. Sister would give us all a dirty look, but Dewey would take on that "offended" look and gaze at one of us, as if he wasn't the culprit. And, in church, he could stop a mass. He would wait until there was a quiet part, when no one was singing or praying, then he'd let it go. Dewey had a real talent.

One night we decided to take Chick's tent to a sandbar not far out in the river. We put the tent, our sleeping bags, clothes, and food into garbage bags and held them over our heads as we swam to the sandbar. On the next trip, we took fishing poles, fry pans, and a metal grate. We set up the tent, gathered firewood, made a fire pit, and placed the grate over it. We had a sack of cooked potatoes to fry, four cans of beans, cooking oil, salt, pepper, and flour for breading the fresh fish fillets.

The plan was to catch fish, clean them, and fry them and the potatoes, heat up the beans, and have supper. We always caught fish so supper would not be a problem.

We fished and fished. At first we had no bites. Just before dark, we got a few bites but we only caught shiners, carp, and red horse suckers.

"We can't eat these things," Dewey wailed. "I'm starved." "Just fish, Dewey. We'll get walleye or catfish soon," I said.

Famous last words!! It was dark and we didn't have a single fish.

"Well," Dougie said, "it looks like we're gonna have potatoes and beans for supper." Well, potatoes and beans were better than nothing, so we began cutting up the potatoes and frying them. Then we opened the beans and dumped them into a pan. Soon the meal was ready and we scooped up the food and ate. The potatoes were gone in a minute and the first batch of beans disappeared quickly, too. Chick opened another can of beans and soon there was a second helping for each of us. What remained, Dewey ate directly out of the pan.

"I'm still hungry," Dewey moaned.

"That's it, Dewey," I said.

"Unless you've got something stashed away, we're done eating for the night," Dougie said.

Dewey moaned and groaned for a while but it did no good.

We sat around the campfire and talked about the stuff thirteen year-old boys talk about. We covered baseball, fishing, and the movies we liked. Finally we were yawning.

"I'm going to bed," I said.

"Yeah! Me, too," Dougie and Chick said. "I'm still hungry," Dewey repeated.

"Go to sleep, Dewey. Then you won't be hungry anymore," Dougie said.

One by one, we undressed and piled our clothes on a log.

We were barefooted, so I cleaned the sand off my feet and climbed into the tent first to my sleeping bag on the far side. Chick followed and crawled into his bag. Then Dewey climbed in. Dougie stripped down to his underwear and put a plastic tarp over our clothes to protect them from possible rain or morning fog. He was the smallest, so he came in last and wiggled into his sleeping bag in the middle. It was a tight squeeze and we were packed in like sardines.

"This tent isn't gonna be big enough for us next summer if we keep growing," Chick said.

"Yeah, Dewey, did you hear that? If you keep growing, we'll have to get a bigger tent," Dougie said.

"FFFFFRRRRRRRRRRTTTTT!!" was Dewey's answer. "Dewey! You pig!" We burst out laughing at Dewey's loud fart. "Does that answer your question, Douglas?" Dewey laughed.

We all chuckled and giggled and finally settled down.

"FFFFFFFFFRRRRRTTTTTTTT!!" The tent rocked with laughter again.

"Dewey, you animal," chided Dougie.

"Dang, Dewey! Put a cork in it," echoed Chick.

"Cripes, Dewey! That one stinks like something you ate a week ago," I blurted.

"You guys are just jealous of my talent," Dewey boasted, and then let another one go. FFFFFFFFFRRRRTTTTT!! We were laughing so hard that tears filled our eyes. And then the odor of the last one hit us.

"Dewey, knock it off. That one was bad," Dougie coughed. FFFFFFFFFFRRRRRRRRRRRTTTTTTTTTTT!! It was a champion! I had never heard one of such long duration in my whole life. We laughed so hard, the tent almost came down. And the smell was unbearable! We took refuge in our sleeping bags, trying to escape, while Dewey basked in total delight.

"C'mon, you guys! Come out for a courtesy sniff," Dewey invited.

The tent smelled like a sewer and Chick was the first to abandon it. "I can't take it," he said, and crawled over Dougie to get fresh air.

"Me, either," chimed in Dougie. I wasn't far behind. We were standing in the cool, night air, shivering in our underwear. Dewey laid there like an old sow, enjoying his stink.

"Dewey, you better go to the other end of the sandbar and make a donation," I said.

"I'm okay now. It's all gone," declared Dewey.

"Oh, sure! We believe that," Dougie said, as he waved the tent flap back and forth in an attempt to air it out.

"C'mon, Dewey! Get out and do your business so we can sleep," ordered Chick.

"I don't gotta go," Dewey announced. "I'm fine now. Come back in. I'll be good."

We didn't have much choice. We surely didn't want to sleep outside so we brushed the sand off our feet and crawled in.

"Now, you be good," Dougie said.

"I will," promised Dewey.

It was quiet for several minutes and then I smelled something nasty again.

"Dewey!" I bellowed.

"Whoops!" Dewey said. "That one was an orphan."

We bawled out Dewey but he just laughed and gave us another blast. He knew we weren't really mad and he always livened up even the dullest time with his talent. I don't know how many times he said "whoops" the rest of the night, but we endured them, laughing and threatening him until we were exhausted and, one by one, we drifted off to sleep.

The next morning, right on cue, Dewey gave us a wake-up blast.

"Next time, no beans for you, Dewey," Dougie said.

"That doesn't make any difference," I said. "He does that on white bread and water."

Dewey laughed, lifted his leg, and another one ripped.

"Whoops."

The Mill Dam

We fished almost daily during the summer. The Gosey was one of our favorite spots, but we also liked fishing in the sloughs, like Gutweiler's and the Cat. Since we had finally convinced our mothers that we could fish in the river and get back alive, we often fished there. And we had another spot that was good for just catching fish if we didn't care what they were.

The Mill Dam was about two miles north of town. It was an easy bike ride that ended with a fast ride down a steep hill and then across a bridge. The hill was the scariest part of the trip. You had to hang on tightly to control the bike so it didn't careen into the ditch.

The Mill Dam had been built long ago to generate electricity. It held back the Mill Creek, making a small lake above the dam. Over the years, the lake had filled in with mud and now there was more mud than water. The lake had a few bluegills, but mostly it had bullheads and carp. Carp fishing was good below the dam. We would dig worms, ride to the dam, and fish opposite the electrical plant. A spring ran over a cement platform, making a little pond. We would make our own small dam with rocks and mud and put our carp there while we continued to fish. At the end of the day we would open our dam, releasing the water and the carp into Mill Creek. We would count the carp as they slid by. On good days, we would catch over two hundred. Since they weren't good to eat, we had no reason to keep them so we did the catch and release thing, over and over. Occasionally, we would catch a catfish or a walleye at this spot.

Sometimes we fished above the dam where we caught bullheads but they weren't as much fun and they had stingers that usually ended up giving one of us a sore hand.

About three inches of water passed over the dam so it was a challenge to walk across it without falling in. Moss and algae made the concrete slippery and we crossed it like tightrope walkers in a circus. At least one of us would generally slide off and go over the edge, but it was an easy swim to the shore if that happened.

One day we found a kayak that somebody had left on the shore above the dam.

"Well, let's take this for a spin," Chick said.

"It's not ours. We better not take it," Dewey replied.

"We won't hurt it; we'll just take it for a ride," Chick said. We finally decided to give it a try and to be very careful.

Chick and Dougie got in and paddled to the pond. It was a fine kayak with waterproofed canvas stretched over a wooden frame. I t flew across the water. Dewey and I watched as they went to the other end of the pond and scared up a few geese and ducks. Finally they came back and pulled up by the shore. "You two gonna try it?"

"Sure," I said. "Get in, Dewey." Off we went. It was great fun paddling. After a while we decided to head back to the shore.

"I think we should take it over the dam," Chick said. "What? Are you crazy?" I said.

Dougie chimed in. "You'll wreck it if you go over the dam." "No way! It'll slide over and go down the creek, just like in the movies," Chick said, excitedly.

"I'm not going," I said.

"Me, either," Dougie said. We all looked at Dewey.

"You go first and if you live, I'll go with you the next time," he said to Chick.

"Okay. Here I go!" Chick said, and he climbed in and paddled to the pond. We ran to the bottom of the dam to watch the show, and to recover Chick's body. He paddled to the dam, lined up the kayak, paddled a few more strokes, and started over the dam. The kayak floated on the top. About five feet of it protruded before it tipped and slid down the face of the dam. There was a rounded ledge at the bottom where the kayak and Chick flew into the air and landed in the water below the dam. Chick held

DAN BOMKAMP

his paddle over his head like an Olympic champion. We cheered, not really believing that he had pulled it off.

"See, I told you," he bragged, as he came to shore. "Let's do it again. I want to go this time," Dewey said. "Okay. Help me carry it back up," Chick said.

Dougie and I stayed at the bottom of the dam. Soon we saw them paddling to the edge of the dam. Dewey was in front and Chick in back. They lined up the kayak and took a couple of strokes toward the dam. This time, the kayak immediately tipped over the edge with Dewey in the front. They flew over the dam and when they got to the ledge, going faster and with more weight in the kayak this time, the kayak hit the water and Dewey went through the bottom of it. With a boy-sized hole in the canvas, the kayak didn't float and Chick ended up going under, too.

Dewey came to the surface. Chick had bailed out. The kayak floated to the top and he grabbed it, and pulled it to shore. Dewey swam over to us, too. "Oops! Looks like the two of us were too heavy for it," he said. The canvas was torn where Dewey had gone through.

"Oh, no! We wrecked it," Chick said.

"It can be fixed," Dougie said. "It needs to be sewn and then waterproofed."

"Let's put it back where we found it and get out of here," Dewey said.

We returned the kayak to its spot. If we had had paper and a pen, we would have left a note explaining that we had wrecked it and were willing to help fix it, but we didn't have a pen or anything to write on. "Well, I guess we'll just leave it and hope for the best," Chick said.

A few days later, Dougie and I were fishing at the Mill Dam and we noticed the kayak was missing. We never did find out who owned it. Well, we were catching carp below the dam when a couple of local guys came driving up, parked, and walked over to us. "How, ya doing, guys?"

"Okay," we answered.

"Whatcha catchin'?" they asked. "Mostly carp."

"Ever get any bullheads?"

"Yeah, some. Why?"

"We're bank-poling and we need bullheads for bait." "Bank-poling?" Dougie asked.

"Yeah! You put a pole in the riverbank, attach a good-sized hook with strong line, and use a bullhead for bait. It works slick for catching those big, flathead catfish."

"Oh, sure! I know about that," I said.

"Well, we need ten bullheads a day and we'll pay a nickel apiece for them."

I looked at Dougie and his eyebrows went up. We were standing about twenty feet from millions of bullheads.

"We might be able to find some for you, Mister," he said. "Great," the man said. "Here, I'll give you my address. If you catch any, bring them over and I'll pay you. In fact, bring all you can catch. I have friends who need them, too." He handed us a piece of paper with his address and said goodbye and left.

"A nickel a bullhead?" Dougie said. "We're rich!" We were so excited that we could hardly reel in our lines fast enough. We ran to the top of the dam and threw our lines in and in a minute we each had a bullhead on the bank. "Wait a minute. What are we gonna do with them? We gotta take them back to town. They won't stay alive on the stringer."

"We'll have to take them in buckets filled with water," I said. We reeled in, put our fishing gear in our bike baskets, and set off for town. As much fun as the hill was to ride down, it was torture to climb. We usually ended up walking our bikes because our legs turned to noodles. Today, however, we were so excited about the bullhead business that we made it to the top in record time.

As we rode down the highway, I said to Dougie, "Should we let Dewey and Chick in on this?"

Dougie looked over at me. "I've been thinking about that, too.

What do you think?"

"Well, they're gonna be real mad if we don't."

He nodded his head. "Yeah! That's what I think, too. We better clue them in. Besides, they're our best friends." It was settled. We would share the millions we would make from our bullhead business with Chick and Dewey.

We stopped at Chick's house. He had been forced to help his mom move the furniture out of the house so the carpeting could be cleaned. He was annoyed because he didn't get to fish. We helped him move the stuff back into the house and got fresh cookies from his mom as a reward. Then we told him about the bullhead business. "A nickel a bullhead! A dollar for every twenty bullheads! We can catch them about as fast as we can pull them in. We're gonna be rich!" He was excited about our new business.

We got on our bikes and rode to Dewey's apartment and found him napping on the couch. "Dewey, we've got a business deal for you," I said. We told Dewey about the bullhead business and he was thrilled.

"Great! Two bullheads and I can get a bag of potato chips; five for a movie, and two for popcorn. What a deal." Good, old Dewey, always thinking about his stomach.

The day was almost shot but we decided to fix up our bikes with buckets for hauling the bullheads. We planned to head to Mill Dam early the next morning to start our new business. We had to figure out how to attach a bucket to our wire baskets. We tried a few ideas, finally settling on cutting an old inner tube into strips which would be tied to the bucket handle, then stretched around the baskets to secure them. This worked well and we were excited about the next day's business. That evening we went to our worm-digging spot and got our supply of bait. We decided to meet at eight o'clock in the morning.

The next morning we were riding merrily along to the Mill Dam. We could hardly wait to get up the hill and coast down the other side. We topped the hill and began the descent, but instead of touching the brakes a tad to slow us down, we let our bikes speed down. Normally we weren't in such a hurry. About halfway down, my front tire began to wobble. It must have been a little crooked and I hadn't noticed it because I had never gone that fast before. Soon the little wobble was a full-blown vibration and the whole bike was shaking. "I can't hold it!" I yelled, as my bike headed for the ditch. I hit the tall grass and weeds and my bike flipped over. I flew over the handlebars and landed in the bushes. My bike did a summersault and landed a short way below me. The rest of the guys couldn't stop, so they continued down the hill. They later ran back to where I was sitting.

"Are you okay?" Dougie asked.

"Yeah, I think so. My bike went nuts and I couldn't control it," I explained.

Chick and Dougie pulled my bike out of the bushes and checked it out. It seemed okay. My fishing pole was missing so we combed the tall grass and Dewey found it. It was intact. We picked up the rest of the stuff and I got on my bike and tried it. It wobbled a bit, but I could ride it. Since I was so close to the bottom and the guys were walking, I decided to walk, too.

We got our fishing gear and the buckets and headed to the pond. We caught bullheads about as fast as we could reel them in. After fishing a few hours, Dewey said, "Let's see how many we got." We agreed that we had enough for one day, so we filled the buckets with fresh water and attached them to our bikes for the ride home.

We soon realized our bikes were off balance with the sloshing water and the buckets were VERY heavy. We had to walk our bikes up the entire hill. "Whew, this isn't as much fun as going down," Dewey said.

"No kidding! Even a crash is more fun than this," I said.

They laughed at my joke.

When we got to the top, we were able to ride again and we were off toward town. We had to proceed slowly so that the water would stay level and not get us off balance. We were almost to town when Dewey lost control and ended up in the ditch. His bullheads were flopping in the grass. "Help me! Rescue my bullheads!" he yelled. We couldn't put our bikes on our kickstands because they were too heavy, so Chick and I held the three bikes while Dougie helped Dewey put the bullheads in the other three buckets.

"There. Now they'll be fine," I said.

Dewey was worried that he had lost his bullheads. "How we gonna know whose bullheads are whose?" he muttered.

"We'll split the money equally," Dougie reassured him.

"Yeah! A four-way split," Chick reiterated.

That made Dewey happy.

We found the man's house. We knocked on his door and told him we had his bullheads. He had a cattle-watering tank set up by his garage and we counted the fish as we plopped them into the tank. Final count was eighty-nine. "You guys don't fool around," the man said, smiling at the nice catch. "I'll let my friends know how expert you are at this and they'll probably want some." We were just about ready to bust. What a business; go fishing and get paid for it! The man gave us $4.45 for our bullheads and told us to bring him whatever we caught.

We rode to the cafe and sat in a booth to divide up our money. "That's a dollar and ten cents each," Dougie said. We divided the money up but there was a nickel left over.

"What should we do with the nickel?" I asked.

"Let's put it away and next time we'll add it to the pot," Dougie said. We decided that Chick should be the treasurer so he took care of the extra nickel. Then we each ordered a coke and an ice cream cone and sat down to savor our well-earned treats.

"This is the best job in the world," Dewey said.

"No kidding! We might be millionaires by the end of the summer," Chick added.

We fished the Mill Dam for the next two weeks. Word got out

that we had a bullhead business and we kept the whole town supplied. One of the men we supplied was my dad's employer and one morning he knocked on our door while I was eating breakfast. There stood Carl with a catfish as big as me. "I thought you might want to see the catfish your bullhead caught," he said. I could hardly speak, let alone close my mouth.

Carl was an average-sized man and he had a big gaff hook in the catfish's lower jaw. The catfish's head was against the back of his shoulder and its tail was dragging on the sidewalk! "Oh, my gosh! Oh, my gosh!" I couldn't believe its size!

"What do you think?" he asked, laughing.

"I think I gotta call my friends and let them see this!" I said, as I ran for the phone. I called the guys and in a couple of minutes they were there, gaping at the trophy sized catfish.

"How much does it weigh?" Dewey asked.

"Where did you catch it?" inquired Chick.

"Did it pull hard?" questioned Dougie. We had lots of questions.

It turned out that he had caught it in the river, about half a mile from the Gosey. "You mean that thing was swimming in the river where we swim?" Dewey wanted to know.

"I think I'll start wearing a swimming suit," Dougie said. We all laughed at Dougie's joke.

The bank-poling season lasted another week and then the fishermen told us that they wouldn't need any more bullheads. But, they said to keep them in mind for next year.

"Well, it was fun while it lasted," I said.

"Yeah! What a way to make money," Dougie said, as we biked toward Chick's house to tell him the sad news that our business got shut down. We called Dewey and he joined us, and for the first day in almost three weeks, we didn't go to the Mill Dam.

"We made over ten dollars each. That's a lot of money," said Dougie, delightfully.

"Sure is. We can buy a lot of good stuff with that," Chick said.

"You know, I'm a little hungry for an ice cream float," Dewey added. We looked at him and laughed.

"An ice cream float does sound good," Dougie said.

"Yeah, no foolin'," I said.

Chick looked at us. "Well, count me in."

We jumped on our bikes and rode to the cafe, pockets full of money; four unemployed business tycoons.

We spent our money wisely and made it last most of the summer. It was the easiest money we had ever earned. Go fishing, and get paid; what a deal!

The Cave

"I think we've caught all the fish that are here," Chick announced.

"Yeah, no kiddin'. We haven't had a bite for an hour," Dougie said.

Dewey was sitting with his feet in the water and we three were lying in the sand watching our fishing poles which were propped up in our pole holders. A pole holder was a forked stick that was stuck into the sand. It supported the fishing pole and you could watch the tip for signs of a bite. The holder also kept the reel above the sand.

We were fishing at the river above the bridge by Snake Island.

Many years earlier there was another bridge that crossed the river and ended at a toll house. The man who owned the bridge collected money from people using the bridge. As cars and trucks became heavier, the toll bridge became inadequate. It was torn down and the new bridge was built about fifty yards downriver. The old piers that held up the toll bridge had mostly washed away with the spring floods, but the one closest to the riverbank had survived. It was a square pile of stones and pilings, and it sat about ten feet from the bank. We made a makeshift bridge of stones from the riverbank to the pier so we could walk across when the water was low. We then fished off the sandy area around the rocks.

Snakes liked the pier so we named it Snake Island.

I was definitely not a snake person. No matter what kind of snake it was, I didn't want it near me. Dewey wasn't as afraid of snakes as I was, but he also would go around them rather than be near them. Chick wasn't afraid of anything. He would pick up almost any repulsive thing, including a snake. But Dougie; he was the snake guy. He loved the things. No matter what size a snake was, he had to pick the dang thing up. If he found a little one, it went into his pocket. One time I was fishing with him at Gutweiler's and he began yelling at me to help him. I thought he had a real emergency so I took off running. There he was, kneeling on the ground by a hole, holding a snake's tail, trying to pull it out of the hole.

"Help me pull this snake out!" he begged.

"Are you nuts? Leave the thing alone. No! Wait. Let me get out of here first, and then let it go!" I said, hightailing it back a safe distance.

Suddenly he flopped backward over into the grass with about a foot of the snake's tail in his hand. T he tail was wiggling and I almost passed out when he held it up to show me. Then a long water snake came to the surface and swam off.

"You're a sick one," I said to Dougie, as he joined me by my fishing pole.

He held the snake tail out to me. "Here, wanna play with it? It won't bite you 'cuz it ain't got a head," he said, laughing.

"I'll take a branch and beat you on the head till you ain't got no head if you come a step closer," I said, in a threatening tone.

He pretended to be scared and threw the snake tail into the water where it wriggled like a live snake until it disappeared under the surface. "You're such a girl when it comes to snakes," he teased.

"Why, thank you. That's the nicest thing you've said to me all day," I said, in a high voice.

Snakes were the only thing that I couldn't stand. Frogs, toads, turtles, lizards, and skinks were fine. But snakes, yikes! Not for me!

Skinks were similar to snakes except they had little legs. Most of the kids called them sand lizards but Dougie and I knew they were skinks. They belonged to the lizard family. They ran back and forth across the sand dunes. We tried to catch them but they were so fast that it was impossible. We wanted to capture a couple to study them, possibly adding them to our zoo. So we devised a plan to catch them. Finally I thought about making a trap. We went to Dewey's dad's restaurant and got a half dozen tomato paste and olive cans. We cut one end out and took them to the sand dunes where we dug holes and put a can in each so that the top was level with the sand. Then we filled sand in around them. Now, when a skink came running past, he would fall into the trap and we could play with it.

Dougie and I buried half a dozen cans and left them overnight. The next morning, we had two skinks. I was pleased at how well my idea had worked, and Dougie was impressed. We trapped skinks for about a week, catching six. We took them to Dougie's and put them in a discarded, leaky aquarium, and we tossed in flies and ants. They seemed happy in their new home but Dougie's dad thought we should return them to their natural habitat, so we did. I enjoyed playing with them, even if they looked like snakes.

Well, we were trying to decide what to do about the fishing situation when Dewey piped up, "Hey guys, have you ever heard of Fisherman's Point?"

"Yeah. It's upriver, isn't it?" Chick commented.

"Yeah. About five miles up, on the other side of the river. My dad says there is good fishing up there," added Dewey.

"Five miles. That's a long way to ride a bike," I said.

"Oh, come on! It's not that far. Besides, if the fish don't bite, there's a cave that we could explore."

"A cave?" we asked.

"Yeah. My dad says counterfeiters hid there long ago." That got everyone's attention, so we packed up our gear, put our poles, tackle boxes, and bait into our baskets and took off across the bridge. We rode on the highway on the north side of the river. It was narrow and had only a minimal shoulder so when cars came past they had to slow down for our bike convoy. We rode on and on and soon we arrived at Fisherman's Point.

We parked our bikes and followed a path to the river. It looked like a good fishing spot. There was an old wing dam that made a current eddy and it seemed to be the perfect place for fish to wait, and for someone to catch them. We spread out along the shore and soon we had our lines in the water. We waited and waited for a bite.

"This is just as bad as at the bridge," Chick wailed.

"Maybe they're just not biting today," Dougie commented.

"Oh, really? You think?" Dewey said. Dougie threw a clod of mud at him.

Dewey stood up and looked at the hill across the highway. He stared and stared and suddenly he said, "Guys, I can see the opening to the cave." We jumped up and ran over by Dewey and looked where he was pointing. Sure enough, way up on the hillside, there was a ledge and a hole.

"Hmm. That's a long way up," Dougie said.

"Yeah! It's almost at the top of the hill," Chick said.

"What's the matter? Can't you girls climb a hill?" Dewey said.

Being compared to a girl was about the worst insult a thirteen year-old boy could tolerate.

"Okay, smart guy! Let's see who's the last one to reach the cave?" Dougie challenged, and he began to climb the trail to the highway. We stashed our fishing gear in our baskets. Each of us had a little flashlight in our tackle box for night fishing or for catching night crawlers on rainy nights, so we grabbed them and hid our bikes in the weeds.

We jumped over the fence and began the climb. Part way up we found a trail that appeared to lead to the cave. It was a good path that weaved back and forth across the hillside until it got to where the hill turned to sheer rock. Then it became very narrow and steep, and we had to continue the incline single file.

"You can sure see for a long way from here," I said.

"No foolin'. And it's a long drop to the bottom," Chick added.

"The fall doesn't scare me. It's the sudden stop at the bottom that hurts," Dougie said, making a joke. We stopped and gazed at the river valley. We could see the church steeple and the water tower in town. The sunlight looked like sparkling diamonds on the surface of the river as it flowed westward to the Mississippi.

We could see its meandering path for miles as it slipped between the tree-lined banks where we fished and swam.

We kept climbing and finally we reached the ledge and the hole in the wall. It was the size of a front door of a house. We couldn't see far inside, but from what we could see, it appeared to be quite large.

"Let's go in," Chick said, always the first one to try something.

"Okay, let's go," Dougie agreed, and they walked in.

Dewey looked at me and we both shrugged; then we went in, too. We walked upright until the cave tapered off, and we had to bend over. We finally caught up to Chick and Dougie who had turned on their flashlights. They were checking out three different openings that branched off from the main cave.

"Looks like it splits here," they observed.

"We'll go left and you two take the middle passage and we'll meet back here," Chick said. We went a short distance and the cave got even smaller and we had to craw1. We continued and soon found ourselves in a good-sized room.

"This is a dead end," Dewey announced.

"Yeah, but look at this room," I said, standing up. "There've been people in here. Look at the ceiling. It's black from fire or candle smoke." There were empty food cans and broken crates and other stuff strewn around.

"Maybe this is where the counterfeiters hid," Dewey said.

"Maybe we'll find some phony money!"

"Yeah, Dewey. I'm sure we're the first ones in here since they were here."

Just then Chick and Dougie came into the room through the little doorway. "Wow, this is better than anything we found," Dougie said. "That other tunnel comes back out on the side of the hill."

"Looks like somebody lived here," Chick said.

"Dewey figures this is where the counterfeiters hung out," I said.

"I think I'd find another job rather than have to live in this
147

place," Chick said. "Let's check out the other tunnel."

We crawled back and down the tunnel to the third cave.

Dougie and Chick led the way and Dewey and I followed. This cave also got smaller and we had to crawl on our hands and knees. The cave floor was clay and we found it to be sticky. Our knees and hands turned red as we made our way through it.

"Maybe we should go back," Dewey said.

"Why, Dewey, are you afraid you'll get your fat butt stuck?" Dougie said.

"I might get nervous and you know what happens when I get nervous, don't you, Douglas?" Dewey warned.

"Oh, no, Dewey! Please don't do that; not in this little space," I pleaded from behind. We laughed and our laughter sounded spooky as it echoed down the cave.

"Whew, that sounds like something out of a horror movie," Dewey said. Then Dewey let one go and it sounded like a bomb going off. We laughed again, but we griped at Dewey as we headed on down the tunnel.

We crawled on and soon my flashlight began to dim. "Hey, guys! My light is almost dead," I said.

"Mine, too," Dewey said, just ahead of me.

"Well, keep up with us. Ours are okay," Chick said.

We crawled on and soon my light went completely out. I could see the light from Dewey's flashlight ahead of me and Dougie and Chick's lights ahead of that. The tunnel continued to get smaller and soon we had to crawl on our bellies. "I don't think I like it in here," Dewey said.

"We don't have much choice, Dewey. We can't back out," I said.

"Just keep going. It's gotta come out somewhere," added Chick.

Suddenly Dewey stopped and I ran smack into him. "My light went out," he said.

"Can you see the other guys?" I asked.

"Just barely," he said. "Hey, guys! Wait up. Our lights are out!"

he yelled.

I couldn't really see much around Dewey but ahead there was a faint light.

"Hurry up, Dewey! We're being left behind!" I urged. Dewey started crawling and soon the faint light disappeared.

"They left us. Those dirty rats," he said. "It's REALLY dark in here."

He was right. I had never been in so much dark. Even on a cloudy night, with no moon or street lights, there's always a little light. But in here it was DARK. I held my hand up but I couldn't see a thing. "We gotta keep moving, Dewey. Just keep crawlin' and we'll find them."

"I can't see anything!" Dewey said, and I could hear panic in his voice.

"Feel ahead with your hand, and keep going. I don't like it any more than you do," I said. "I'm here with you. I won't leave you."

I could hear and feel Dewey moving forward so I began to crawl ahead. We moved slowly down the cave in complete darkness. Every so often I would get too close to Dewey and his feet would kick me in the face. The walls and roof of the cave were so close that our sides and back rubbed on them. "If this gets much smaller, I'm gonna get stuck," Dewey said. I didn't even want to think about what it would be like going backward out of this place.

"It can't get much smaller or the other guys would have got stuck," I said.

"Yeah! When we catch up to them, I'm gonna pound a knot or two on their heads for leaving us," Dewey said.

I don't know how far we crawled, but suddenly I could feel fresh air on my face. "Dewey, do you feel that air?" I asked.

"Yeah, I can. We must be almost out, thank God!" he said.

We crawled faster and we could see light ahead and smell the warm, fresh air. We reached the opening and emerged into the sunshine. It took a few minutes for our eyes to adjust to the brightness, but there sat Dougie and Chick smiling at us. They were covered with red clay.

"You rats! How come you left us?" I said.

"We thought you were behind us till we got to the end," Dougie said.

"Yeah, sure! I'm sure you did," Dewey mocked.

"We did," Chick said. "We were surprised when it took you so long to come out."

"We thought maybe Dewey had farted in there and both of you got gassed," Dougie said, laughing. We laughed and even Dewey thought it was funny.

"Well, let's climb down and go home," I said. "I've had enough cave exploring for one day." Dewey looked at me and began laughing.

"What's so funny?" I asked.

"You've got a shoe print on your face," he said, laughing like mad. The other two looked and began laughing.

"A perfect print of Dewey's shoe," Chick said.

"Well, better that than a butt print. I came close to that a couple of times," I said.

We laughed and talked all the way down the hill. It had been a good adventure but I don't think any of us was in a big hurry to explore any more caves for a while.

We got back to our bikes and began the long ride home. Cars passed us and some passengers laughed when they saw us. I suppose four boys covered with red clay looked peculiar riding along with bikes loaded down with fishing gear. We didn't care. What had begun as a boring fishing day had turned into another exciting adventure.

Treasures For Our Moms

St. John the Baptist Church had an annual summer festival. We looked forward to this time and this particular year it was going to be better because we had money to spend. Our bullhead business was financing our fun. We each made a point to save several dollars for the event and our parents usually chipped in a few bucks. We were flush with money and would be able to take in all the sights.

A major portion of the money would be used for food. In addition to the usual hotdogs and hamburgers, there was the lady who sold cotton candy, popcorn, caramel corn, and candy apples from a trailer decked with colored lights. We spent much time there. The lady was kind and we were fascinated by the strands of cotton candy that hung from her hairnet like wisps of tiny pink or blue clouds. We tried her sweet and salty treats. I especially liked the snow cones. They were served in pointed cups and a sweet syrup was drizzled over the top. I loved them in spite of the brain freezes I got from them. Chick favored the candy apples, and Dougie went for the caramel corn. Dewey loved the cotton candy and swore that the blue tasted better than the pink. He usually wore half a serving on his face and eyebrows.

We always spent money at the dunk tank. The church rented the apparatus and people were lured to sit on a board suspended over a tank of water. Game participants paid twenty-five cents for five baseballs to throw at a target on the side of the tank. If the target was hit, the person on the board dropped into the water with a big splash. It was great entertainment. We always hoped that Sister Henry or another sister would volunteer, but they never did. The closest we came to that kind of thrill was when we managed to drown a couple teachers from Dougie's school.

Then there were the games that yielded prizes. One challenge involved throwing hoops, or wooden rings, over prizes displayed on a low table in the middle of a game tent. If the ring landed around the prize and fell to the table, you won the item. How difficult could that be?

But we watched the game and noticed that no one was winning. "Hey, Mister. How do we know those rings will fit over those prizes?" Dougie inquired.

"Here, watch this," the man said, and he dropped a ring over one of the prizes and it fell to the table. "You have to do it just right," he said, smiling at us. "Six rings for a quarter. How many do you want?"

We were challenged. We huddled and decided to try to get a better deal. "How many do you get for more money?" Chick asked.

"Fifteen rings for fifty cents, or thirty-five rings for a dollar," the man answered.

"Thirty-five for a dollar! Let's pool our money and we'll have lots more chances," Chick figured out. We bamboozled the man by each giving Chick a quarter and he was then able to buy thirty-five rings. We divided them up, each getting nine, except Dougie, who settled for eight. What a deal-nine rings for a quarter!

The table had some interesting things on it. A block in the middle displayed a gold watch. Another block held a genuine leather wallet and still another had a fancy hunting knife. Around the edges of the table were blocks with lesser prizes, but we didn't care-a prize was a prize, and we intended to get lots of them.

We spread out around the tent and pushed as close to the plank as possible, took careful aim, and tossed our rings. Mine hit the edge of a block and bounced off the table onto the ground. Dougie's hit a block but hung on the edge, and Chick's fell between two blocks on the table. Dewey's ring hit a block, looped around it, and came to rest on the table. A winner! "Hey, hey! There's a prize going out to this young man!" the man announced. He picked up Dewey's ring and reached into a box under the counter and handed Dewey something that looked like an open-ended straw tube.

"What the heck is this thing?" Dewey questioned, as he turned the prize over and over in his hands.

"It's a Chinese Finger Trap," the man said. "Put a finger in each end and then you're trapped."

Dewey put his index finger in each end and then tried to pull them out. The woven straw tube contracted and his fingers were stuck. "Hey! This is cool," Dewey said, as he pulled and tugged, trying to free his fingers. We laughed at Dewey and his prize, and he finally figured out that if he pushed to loosen it, his fingers would slip out.

We took another turn and this time I got a ringer. "Hey, another prize!" the man shouted. He handed me a pair of chopsticks.

"Gee, thanks. Now if I ever go to China, I'll be able to eat," I said, looking at the crappy prize. Next round Chick got one of those finger trap things and Dougie won a whistle that unrolled like a snake when you blew, then rolled up again. Dewey got a Hawaiian necklace on the next round. We won prizes but they were just crap; all junk prizes. We had used most of our chances.

"Hey, Mister, let's see you drop a ring around the watch," Dougie said.

"What? Don't you guys trust me?" the man asked. "No," Dougie snapped.

The man took a ring out of his apron pocket and dropped it over the watch. It whirled around the block and dropped to the bottom. "See? You just need to know how to toss the ring," the man said, picking up the ring and shoving it back into his apron pocket.

"You're right," Dougie said. "I have one ring left. Would you mind trading rings with me?"

A worried look came over the man's face. "Just throw the ring, kid. They're all the same."

"Well, if they're the same, let me use that one," Dougie said.

"Hey, look guys. There's our friend Mr. Audetta, the policeman. Let's see if he thinks I should get the ring of my choice," Dougie said.

The man moved over by Dougie. "Here, kid! Take the ring. You have to hit the target anyway, so what's the difference?" Dougie smiled. Then he took careful aim and tossed the ring. It hit the watch block and caught on the edge, rolled to the side, and then dropped over the block and landed on the table.

"Ok, I'll have the watch," Dougie said. Strangely, the man didn't announce the win, but he looked rather sick as he picked up the ring. He reached into a box under the counter and took out a little black box with a watch and handed it to Dougie.

"Here. Now beat it," were his words.

"Oh, Mister," Chick said. "I want to try Dougie's lucky ring for my last chance."

Mr. Audetta was now standing nearby and watching. The man traded rings for Chick's last toss. Chick repeated Dougie's throw and won a watch. Of course, Dewey and I weren't going to let a chance like this get by us, so we both requested the lucky ring in turn. A few minutes later the four of us were walking across the carnival grounds sporting our sparkling new; gold watches. Mr. Audetta walked with us, listening to our story about how we had figured out the man's scam. He smiled and laughed and told us to have fun as he walked toward the hot dog stand.

We were proud of ourselves, so we decided to try another game, similar to the last one, except that the table had a display of dishes. There were glasses, plates, bowls, and larger dishes. The object of the game was to throw a nickel at a dish and if it landed in the dish, you won it. That shouldn't be too tough to pull off. Others were already playing the game, so we spread out to see if we could uncover any trick. After watching for a while, we could see that it was more difficult than it looked. The glasses were small targets and if you tried for a plate, the nickel seemed to glance off and land on the table or slide off to the ground. We huddled and talked it over.

"I think putting a spin on the nickel might be the trick," Dougie said.

"Line it up so it will glance off one dish, which will slow it down, and it will land in the dish behind," Chick said.

"Aim good," Dewey said.

We got our nickels and spread out. Dougie was the first to win a dish with his spinning-nickel technique. Then I got one; then Chick, and then Dougie. Dewey got a big bowl. We were getting dishes one after another. The poor man could hardly keep up with us. He was losing prizes faster than he could count. We flipped nickels for a half hour and collected a stack of dishes.

"Our moms will be delighted," Chick said.

"No kiddin'. We'll be in good with them for months," Dougie said. The man was helpful and gave us each a box for hauling our dishes since he had many empty ones by the time we were finished.

"It wouldn't hurt my feelings if you guys didn't come back," he grumbled.

"Okay, Mister. Thanks for all the dishes," I said.

The dishes were in orange and pink hues; shiny and fancy.

Since we had won so much loot, we decided to take our prizes home before the evening events. My mom was so surprised. She stacked the dishes away in the cupboard and said she intended to use them on special occasions because they were so elaborate. I was indeed proud of myself.

We met up again at suppertime and ate hot dogs and a hamburger each, and then we topped the meal off with a candy apple and a snow cone. The playground at St. John's was packed with people and music filled the air along with the mouth-watering aromas of food and carnival treats.

"How did your mom like the dishes?" I asked the guys. "Great!" Dougie said. "She's going to use them at holidays and stuff."

"Mine, too," Chick said.

"Yeah! My mom thought they were too special for everyday use," said Dewey. "Guess they are all taking extra good care of them."

We had one last game to try. This tent had a table in the middle with a display of small glass bowls filled with water and each bowl had a goldfish swimming around. If you could toss a ping-pong ball into a bowl, you won the fish. We bargained for a good deal on balls and we had great fun winning fish for the next hour or so. By the time we ran out of money and balls, we each had a plastic bag with a half dozen goldfish.

We took our fish home and got them settled. Then we went back to St. John's and strolled around the playground, talking to our friends, and showing off our new watches. Soon it was time for the festival to close. There was a chill in the air when we headed to our bikes.

"Want to sleep out tonight?" I said.

"Yeah, let's sleep out," Dougie said.

"Sure, let's," Dewey said.

"Count me in," Chick agreed.

We rode to my house and the guys called their parents to inform them of our plan and then we crawled into the tent. Our sleeping bags were stretched out, ready to go, so we quickly settled in. It had been a long day but we had done well for ourselves.

"We really fixed that guy with the watches," Dougie laughed. "That was pretty smart of you to figure out that his ring was bigger," I said.

"Yeah, Dougie. Thanks for the new watch," Dewey said. "Yeah, thanks," we all chorused. We talked and laughed, and Dewey added a little noise to the conversation, and it wasn't long until we drifted off to sleep-four tired boys with four new watches, and four happy moms with cupboards full of fancy dishes.

It's funny though, as I think back, I don't remember my mom ever using those dishes. Maybe she thought they were too pretty to use, or maybe she forgot where she put them.

Boy Scouts

Dewey, Chick, and I were in my backyard throwing shelled corn to my chickens and pigeons when Dougie rode in, knees flying. He slammed on his brakes, throwing up a dust cloud and loose gravel. "What's your hurry?" Dewey said, fanning the dust away.

"Did you guys hear about the Boy Scout troop that's gonna start?" Dougie announced, excitedly.

"No. Are you sure?" I asked.

"Yeah! There's a meeting next week. My dad saw it in the newspaper," Dougie said, producing a folded copy from his back pocket. We gathered around, spread the paper out, and began reading.

"Local Boy Scout Troop Being Organized," the headline read. Dougie began, "There will be a meeting next Monday at the Municipal Building to organize a Boy Scout troop for the area. Local boys, ages 12 and up, are invited to attend the meeting and if there is enough interest, a new Scout troop will be formed." The article went on to explain the scouting program and it gave the time and other information.

"Wow! How cool! We would get uniforms and do all kinds of neat stuff in the Boy Scouts," Dewey said.

"Yeah! They get merit badges and stuff. Let's go," Chick said.

We agreed. That evening we talked to our parents about financing us in the Boy Scouts. Of course, what parent would say no to a boy who wanted to be a Scout?

We rode to the Municipal Building on the evening of the meeting. As we arrived, two of the town's biggest bullies rode up on their bikes. They were a year older than we were. Immediately, Roger came over and began to pester Dewey.

"Hey, fat boy! Your pants look like they're gonna fall off," he said, as he grabbed Dewey's pants and pulled them almost up to his armpits.

"Cut it out, you puke!" Dewey said.

"Oooh , I'm scared of you," Roger mocked, letting go of Dewey. Dewey adjusted his pants and then pulled the wedgie out of his backside. Then Mike, the other bully, grabbed my bike and took off with it. He rode fast, then slammed on the brakes and made a skid mark. "Cut it out! You're gonna ruin my tires!" I yelled. He laughed and continued his sport of wearing down my tires. I took off after him, yelling, just as Roger started for Dougie's bike, planning to do the same thing, when Mr. McQuillan, who was going to be the Scout leader, came out of the building.

"You guys get off those bikes!" he yelled at Mike and Roger.

They stopped and came back. "Do those bikes belong to you?" he asked.

"No, but these guys don't care if we use them," Mike said, looking at us and giving us a warning glance.

"The heck we don't," said Chick. "These boneheads think they can pick on anyone. They come on like tough guys. Let's see how tough you are," he said, walking toward Mike. Chick wasn't scared of anybody.

"Hold it! Nobody's gonna show anybody anything. Do you guys want to be Scouts, or not?" We were mad as heck but we wanted to be Scouts, so we backed down, and Mike and Roger laughed and walked into the building.

There was much interest in a scouting program so a troop was organized that night. We paid our dues and were sworn in. Mike and Roger joined, too, but I think they wanted membership just to gain access to more victims to bully.

We met every Monday evening and we soon had a fun group, with the exception of Mike and Roger, who didn't pitch in. We would work on merit badges and projects and then Mike and Roger would show up in time to share in the credit. I think Mr. McQuillan was wise to their strategy but he didn't say anything.

One Monday, Mr. McQuillan told us we were going to have a camp out at the Mill Dam. Although the four of us slept out most nights anyway, it would be great fun to camp in a big group. We gathered tents and gear and we met at the Municipal Building the following Friday afternoon. After loading our gear onto several pickup trucks, we set off for the Mill Dam. There was a picturesque flat meadow on the other side of the Mill Pond that made a great camping site. We pitched our tents, gathered rocks for a fire pit, and got our campsite organized. The canoes were brought off the trucks and a few guys paddled them across the pond so they would be ready for canoeing the next day. That evening we roasted hot dogs and had pop, chips, and S'mores. Then we sat around the campfire and told stories, laughed, and had a great time.

Typically, Mike and Roger didn't join in. They sat to the side and made smart remarks about the stories we were telling and joked about some of the kids. "Why don't you two get in your tent and shut up?" I said. Roger glared at me, but the rest of the guys backed me, and soon he and Mike walked off to their tent. Our Scout leaders decided to go to bed, too, and told us to make sure the fire was out when we turned in. "And, don't get into trouble."

"Who, us?" we thought to ourselves.

We waited until everything quieted down and then we huddled together and spoke, "Any of you guys sick and tired of Mike and Roger?" Chick whispered.

"Yeah! We're all sick of them," said a kid who had his S'mores "borrowed" by Mike.

"I think it is time for a lesson," I said. "What are we gonna do?" another kid asked. "Here's the idea," Dougie said.

We shared the plan that Dewey, Dougie, Chick, and I had devised upon learning of the camp out at the Mill Dam. Of course, we knew the area so well that it was easy to think of something. Everyone agreed, so we crept to Mike and Roger's tent and listened. We knew they were sleeping by their breathing. Dewey sat down, took off his shoes and socks, and then he, Chick, and two other big guys crawled into the tent.

"Now!" Chick whispered, and two boys jumped on the sleeping bullies; Dewey and Chick on top of Mike, and Charlie and Ben on top of Roger. One guy shoved a sock into the mouth of each victim. By this time, their mouths were open to shout, so the socks went in easily. The rest of us then jumped into the tent and held them down. They were mad, cussing at us through the socks.

Once they were pinned down, we took rope and tied them up, like a couple of hogs, and carried them to the shore of the Mill Pond. We put them into one of the canoes and the rest of us got into the other canoes and paddled to the middle of the pond. We towed Mike and Roger's canoe behind. When we got to the middle, we stopped and Dougie stood up in his canoe.

"Mike and Roger, you guys are bullies and lazy and we don't want you in our Boy Scout troop."

The two of them, mad as heck, were trying to break free from the ropes and spit out the socks that were in their mouths.

"I now call a vote. Boy Scout troop 133 will decide if you can remain members," Dougie spoke in an official manner.

One by one, each member had his say. "It is unanimous," Dougie announced, "You are hereby voted out of the troop."

"Punishment is due!" Dewey said.

"What is the punishment for being a bully?" Dougie said.

"Drown them!" the littlest kid in the troop said.

"Any other ideas?" Dougie asked. "Okay. It seems that the troop has spoken; drowning it will be."

By now, Mike and Roger had quieted down and were looking scared. "Mo may," Mike said.

"What's that? No way?" Dougie said, and smiled evilly.

"Way."

We moved our canoes close enough to slightly tip Mike and Roger's canoe and it began to take in water. They whined and cried as they got wet and their canoe was sinking lower and lower in the water. We were silent and staring, then we tipped the canoe over, and the two bullies went into the water. We grabbed their canoe and took it with us as we paddled back.

Then, from a distance, we laughed and laughed as they sat in fifteen inches of water. Dewey, Chick, Dougie, and I knew that there was only a little water in the pond, and lots of mud, but Mike and Roger didn't know that. They thought they were going to the bottom. They began wriggling out of their ropes, trying to stand up and come after us, but they sank to their knees in the mud. The farther they came toward us, the deeper they went into the mud, and finally they were in up to their waists. Mike managed to get his hands loose and he untied Roger. They pulled the socks out of their mouths and began shouting threats of murder at us. We hurried back to our tents and pretended to be asleep. Soon their noise awakened the leaders.

Mr. McQuillan walked to the edge of the pond and shined his flashlight onto the water. By now, we all had come out of our tents, yawning, and stretching. The flashlight caught Mike and Roger, and they looked like a couple of creatures from the Black Lagoon. They were covered from head to toe with the black, stinky mud and were crawling toward the shore.

"What do you two think you're doing? You didn't have permission to go swimming," Mr. McQuillan said.

"Swimming? You think this looks like swimming?" Roger screamed.

"Those little snots tried to drown us!" Mike yelled.

We all looked at each other like we had no idea what was going on.

"You're trying to blame your foolishness on these boys? Get in here, you're confined to your tent for the night, and I'm taking you back to town first thing in the morning. You're out of the troop."

"But, they …. But, but … " was all they could mutter.

"No excuses. You were swimming without permission. You're out of here," was the reply.

We hustled back to our tents and laughed and giggled for an hour. We could hear Mike and Roger trying to "de-mud" and cussing us for the prank we had pulled.

The next morning, we watched as Mr. McQuillan made Mike and Roger take their tent down and pack up their stuff. Everything they owned was coated in mud. Mike and Roger were still covered with the stuff but, by this time, it had dried and they made a lot of dust as they worked. They packed up and began hiking up the hill to the other side of the pond. An assistant leader was to haul them back to town. "Bye, boys," someone shouted. They didn't even turn around. Mr. McQuillan stayed with us.

"Well, gentlemen, how about breakfast?" he asked. "That sounds good! We're famished," Dewey said.

"Why so hungry? You guys just slept all night, didn't you?" he said, smiling.

"Uh, yeah, sure! We went to bed and fell asleep, immediately," Dougie said.

"That's what I thought. You know, Mike and Roger said you guys tried to drown them. What a story!" we all laughed. Yeah! What a story!

"What a story! How could they have possibly drowned in twelve inches of water?" Dougie said.

Mr. McQuillan smiled. He knew what had gone on and was probably glad to be rid of Mike and Roger, too.

Our troop was much improved after their departure and we spent many great weekends camping and working on our merit badges. Mike and Roger never bothered us again. I think they feared the whole bunch would come against them and they weren't so sure that we would dump them in shallow water next time around.

A Full Day of Fun?

Dewey came down the alley and pulled his bike up next to the picnic table where I was sorting through stuff in my new tackle box. My grandparents had visited over the weekend, and good, old gramps had brought me this as a gift. He worked at the Coast to Coast store and he always brought me the latest in fishing gear from the fishing department. I was a lucky guy because I was the first grandson. The tackle box was shiny and beautiful. Gramps had included a roll of cork sheeting which could be cut into small pieces and placed in the bottom of the various compartments to separate and protect the lures and stuff It also made my tackle box look really cool.

"Nice tackle box! Where did you get it? Your grandpa?" questioned Dewey.

"Of course. You don't think I've got money to buy something like this, do you?" I said.

"I wish my grandpa worked at a fishing store," Dewey said. "What ya gonna do today?" he asked.

"Chick and Dougie are coming over and we're gonna wash my mom's car," I said. "Then, we'll probably fish."

Just then Chick and Dougie rode into the yard. "Wow! Neat!" Dougie said, as he examined my new treasure. "Grandpa?"

"Yup."

"Cool! Now we got all the tackle we need. We won't have to use our tackle boxes," Chick said.

"Think again. You guys aren't gonna use my stuff," I said, closing the box and latching the top.

"You guys ready to wash the car?" They were, so I went into the house and told mom we were ready to start. "I'll drive it to the backyard," I said.

"What? I don't think so," she said.

"Oh, come on! I know how to drive. It's only around the corner," I begged.

"Okay, but the rest of those outlaws can't ride with you," she instructed.

She tossed me the keys and I ran out the door.

"You guys get the hose out and put water in that pail while I drive around to the backyard," I said.

"What? You get to drive it?" the guys wondered.

"Sure. It's no big deal," I said, like it was an everyday thing.

"Just stay out of the way," I said.

"I'll be in the tree," Chick said. We all laughed at Chick's joke.

I ran to the street and got into the car. I rolled down the window, adjusted the seat, tilted the mirrors, and got situated in the seat. I turned the key and found a cool song on the radio, so I turned up the volume to a deafening level. Then I signaled, looked over my shoulder to check for traffic, and put the car into drive. I cruised about fifty feet to the corner, stopped, signaled a right turn, turned, went about fifty yards, stopped, and signaled a right turn. I went another fifty feet to our yard and stopped, and just to be safe, I signaled a right turn and drove into the backyard.

Dewey and Dougie were sitting on the picnic table watching, and Chick was gazing down from the tree. I drove up to the picnic table, put the brakes on, and put the car in park. Then I turned off the ignition and, just for good measure, I blew the horn to signal my arrival.

Dewey and Dougie gave me a good hand clapping and Chick jumped down and yelled, "Bravo!"

"That was cool," Dewey said. "You gonna drive it back to the front when we're done?"

"Probably," I said, "It's no big deal." They were real impressed with my driving abilities, and so was I.

We were washing the car and soon Chick splashed a sponge full of soapy water on Dewey. Dewey grabbed the hose and shot water at Chick, who ran behind Dougie, who ended up getting wet. "You bonehead!" Dougie yelled, as he threw a soaked sponge at Dewey. Dewey dropped the hose and ducked behind the car when he saw the sponge coming. I grabbed the hose. I sprayed Chick and chased Dewey around the yard. Chick picked up the hose, bent it in half, and cut off my water supply. There was a still a dribble of water so I swung it back and forth, splashing at least some water at him. He raised his arm to protect himself, and the metal end on the hose nailed him on the elbow.

Chick stood there looking goofy for a second and then he dropped the hose and fell over on his face. I thought he was pretending to be dead so I soaked him good with the hose. He didn't move.

"Is he hurt?" Dougie shouted. I stopped the squirting business and he still laid there in the grass, like he was dead.

"Oh man, you killed him," Dewey said. "I only hit him in the arm," I said.

We rolled Chick over. His eyes were half closed, but he was breathing.

"He's not dead. I think he's knocked out," Dougie said. "How can he be knocked out? He got hit in the arm," I said. Chick began to move and his eyes opened. "What happened to me?" he muttered.

"You got knocked out," Dewey said.

Chick moved his arm back and forth and let out a yelp. "Ow! My elbow hurts like heck." We helped him to the picnic table.

"Do you remember me hitting you in the arm?" I asked. "Yeah. Then I heard a high-pitched noise in my ears and everything went black. Did you hose me while I was knocked out?" he asked, looking at his wet clothes.

"Yeah, sorry. I thought you were pretending to be dead," I confessed.

"You must have hit a nerve and caused him to pass out," Dougie said.

"Cool! I never saw anybody pass out before," Dewey said. "Well, I'm okay now. Let's finish up but no more water fights," Chick said.

"If I remember right, you were the one that started the water fight," I said. Chick shrugged his shoulders and grinned.

We finished the car and I made a big deal over driving it back to the street in front of the house. It was a grand affair, and I parked it carefully against the curb and returned the keys to mom.

Since it was lunchtime, mom brought a tray of food to the picnic table. She had a stack of sandwiches, chips, cookies, and Kool-Aid. It didn't take long for the food to disappear and the guys left to get their fishing gear, and then we headed for the Gosey.

It was our standard practice to fish either above or below the swimming hole because we thought it wasn't a good idea to have fish hooks stuck in roots and logs in the water where we swam, especially after witnessing the incident with Johnny and the Daredevil earlier in the summer.

The remnants of an old fence stopped abruptly the edge of the river. It was easy to climb, so when we fished there, we just stepped over it. I was above the fence fishing and had caught a few nice bluegills when Dewey came up. He threw his bobber and hook but it caught in a tree. "Dang, I'm hung up," he said. He pulled and shook his pole, and finally the hook, sinker, and bobber broke off He laid his pole in the grass and climbed over the fence to replace his lost tackle. As he stepped over, the crotch of his shorts caught on the top of the fence and he ripped his pants open. "Jeez! My mom will kill me. These shorts are new," he whined. He picked up my tackle box and was carrying it back.

"Hey, why are bringing my box? Don't you have anything in your box?" I said.

"I'm out of bobbers. You'll lend me one, won't you, good buddy?" he begged.

When Dewey got to the fence, instead of stepping over like we always did, he swung out over the river at the end of the fence. He held on to the end fence post and swung around it.

When he was halfway around, the arm holding my tackle box smacked against the fence post and the tackle box latch flew open. The contents hit the water and the little pieces of cork sheeting were floating on the surface.

"Yikes!" screamed Dewey.

I looked up to see my box hanging from his hand, open, and upside down. I ran over and saw the little pieces of cork floating down the river along with my bobbers and floating lures. My *Bass o Reno, Hula Popper, and Rapalas* were going down the river and the rest of my stuff was on the river bottom.

"Dewey! You idiot! You dumped all my stuff in the river!" I was ready to strangle him.

"I didn't do anything. It had a bad latch," he said, defensively and he climbed back to the other side of the fence.

Just then Dougie and Chick came running up and they took off their shoes and jumped into the river to collect the lures and cork pieces that were floating away. I looked into the water; it was pretty shallow and most of the heavy stuff was on the bottom.

"Get your shoes off and help me gather up the stuff," I said to Dewey. We worked together for about fifteen minutes. Dougie and Chick had the floating things and returned them to the tackle box.

"Whew, it looks like we got it all," Dewey said, cheerfully.

"Yeah, that's great, Dewey. Remember how nice the box looked before you put your meat hooks on it? Now look. It's a disaster!" I said.

"You're too fussy about your tackle box. Mine looks like this all the time," Dewey said.

I grabbed for him but Dougie stopped me.

"C'mon. It was an accident. I'll help you sort it out tomorrow," he promised. Good, old Dougie. He was always the peacemaker.

"Well, we might as well fish a while yet," Chick said. We took our poles and climbed the fence. We had probably scared the fish away so we needed to move upriver. Dougie cast a red and white Daredevil near a brush pile. He had turned his reel only a few turns when a good-sized fish boiled at his lure and grabbed it. "I got one!" he yelled. His drag was screaming out and he played the fish like an expert. We could see it was a big dogfish. "Oh boy! A dog," Dougie said.

Dogfish were about the ugliest fish in the river, but they were strong and fighting.

"Be careful. He's hooked loosely," I said. The hook was barely caught in the lip.

"I'll bring him in close and you grab him and toss him on the bank," Dougie said.

I stretched out on the bank and got ready. As the fish got close enough for me to reach, he made a big splash and tried for deeper water. When he pulled against the hook, it popped free and flew over my head. "Dang! He came off," I said. "It's a good thing I was lying down or I'd have that hook in my head," I said, as I got to my feet.

I turned around and looked at Dougie staring at his right forearm. The Daredevil had snapped in the air and had landed on him, and two of the three hooks were imbedded in his arm.

"Jeez, Dougie! Are you okay?" I panicked.

Dougie stared at the hooks and then looked at me. "Um, I've been better. As you can see, I have a Daredevil in my arm." He was very calm.

"Does it hurt?" I asked, awkwardly.

"Yup, like real bad."

"Hey, guys! Come here. Dougie's hooked," I yelled to Chick and Dewey.

"Wow! That must hurt," Dewey sympathized.

"No crap, Sherlock! What was your first clue?" Dougie said.

We snickered at that but it wasn't funny to see Dougie in so much pain.

"Cut the line, and let's take a look at it," Chick said. I got out my pocketknife and carefully cut the line. Dougie grimaced in pain as I touched the Daredevil.

"Whew, that's really stuck in. Maybe we should see a doctor," I said.

"Let me see," Chick said. He took Dougie's arm and carefully looked at it and touched the hook to see how deeply it was lodged. Dougie gritted his teeth but he didn't pull away.

"See if you can move the hook," Dougie said. Chick took it and pulled it backward slowly.

"It won't come out. It's in past the barb," he said. "Try pushing it all the way through," Dougie said. Chick looked at him. "Are you sure?"

"Yeah, go ahead and try it," repeated Dougie.

Dewey was turning white and wobbling around like he was going to pass out. "Sit down Dewey. We don't need you to faint and fall in the river. Then we would need a crane to haul you out."

Chick pushed the hook so you could see the points just under the skin. Dougie gasped but didn't say stop, so Chick kept pushing. The skin came up to two little points that first turned red and then white and then the points of two hooks popped through. Dougie let out his breath, and so did the rest of us. "Okay, push them till the barb is through," Dougie said. Chick began pushing again and soon the barbs were out. We all breathed again. Dougie looked at me. "Can you cut the barbs off with your pliers?" As much as I wanted to say no, I nodded my head and got the pliers from my tackle box. "Now, push them up so he can cut them," Dougie said to Chick and me. Dewey turned his head. He didn't want to look.

I put the side cutter of the pliers on the first hook point and applied pressure. I heard Dougie take a deep breath and hold it, and I squeezed the pliers and the hook point popped off. One down. We took a breather and wiped the sweat off our foreheads. I gripped the other barb and cut it off. Chick backed the hooks out of Dougie's arm.

"Whew!" we sighed simultaneously.

Dougie grinned at us. "Well, you two should be doctors."

"No way! I about puked when those hooks came through," Chick said.

"Me, either. That is the only operation I ever want to do," I said.

Dewey looked up from the ground and shook his head. "I don't think that would be a good idea for me, either, I'd probably pass out every time I saw blood." We all laughed at Dewey.

Surprisingly there wasn't much blood on Dougie's arm. Just a couple of holes with a little bleeding. He worked his fingers back and forth and all seemed to be okay. "Well, I guess I'm ready to fish again, but my Daredevil is ruined," he laughed.

"I'll lend you one of mine, but I'm not going to fish next to you," I said.

We spent another couple hours fishing and talking and laughing. It was close to suppertime and so we headed home. Chick dropped off first. "Later, guys," he said, as he turned down his street. Next came Dewey. He turned off and waved.

"See ya guys tomorrow?" and Dewey signed off.

"Yeah, Dewey. Tomorrow it is," we answered.

We came to Dougie's house. We stopped in front. "Well, thanks for fixing my arm," he said.

"No problem, pal. I don't think I could have done what you did, letting us push that hook through," I said.

"I knew you guys could do it. You're my best friends and friends do their best for each other." He punched me in the shoulder. We grinned, and I punched him back. "I'll come over and help you sort your tackle box tomorrow morning," he said, and he pulled into his yard. "See ya," and he waved.

"See ya, Dougie," I replied.

I rode the two blocks to my house feeling pretty good. What started out simple had become pretty crazy, but it all worked out in the end. With friends like Dougie, Dewey, and Chick, every day was a memorable adventure.

One Potato, Two Potatoes

I was feeding my critters as Dougie rode up. "Hey, you want a job?" he said, as he skidded to a stop.

"What job?" I asked.

"My dad was at the grocery store and heard they want to hire a few kids to sort potatoes."

"Sort potatoes?" I asked.

"Yeah! They'll pay $2.50 an hour," he stated.

"Great! At $2.50 an hour, we'd be rich in no time! You bet! Let's go," I said, eagerly.

"I've called Dewey and Chick and they're gonna meet us at the store," Dougie said, getting on his bike. I ran to the house and told my mom I was going to the grocery store to work and that I would be back later. Then Dougie and I rode uptown.

About a block from the store, I began to notice a terrible smell. "Whew, what's that?" I choked.

"Jeez, I don't know, but it smells rotten," Dougie said. We rode on and the stench became stronger. As we rounded the corner by the grocery store, we could see a semi parked at the back of the store. Dewey and Chick were standing by the truck, looking inside.

"Dewey, is that smell you?" Dougie yelled. Dougie and I began laughing at his joke.

"Not quite, Douglas, but why don't you come here and take a look?" Dewey said.

Dougie and I parked our bikes and walked over. The doors were open and the truck was piled to the ceiling with burlap bags full of potatoes. The smell was incredible; like a road-killed raccoon that had been sun-dried for a week. "We have to sort these potatoes?" I asked.

The store owner put his head out the back door. "You guys want to work?" he inquired.

"What is the job?" Chick said.

"Some of these potatoes have spoiled so we're going to dump them into several cow-watering tanks, wash and sort them, and bag up the good ones. I'll pay you $2.50 an hour," he offered.

"This whole truckload?" Dougie asked. "Yep!" he stated.

We looked at each other and Dewey spoke up. "Okay, I guess we'll do it." We nodded.

The owner left and soon came back with a pickup truck loaded with three cow tanks. We pulled them off the truck and placed them on the ground behind the semi. "We'll fill these tanks with water, then dump the potatoes in this one, sort out the good ones, and put them in the second tank. Then you guys can wash them off and put them into the third tank for rinsing before the final bagging. Any questions?" he asked.

We didn't have any, so he began filling the tanks with a hose and we climbed into the back of the semi and began to pass the bags of potatoes out the back door of the trailer. The smell was so strong, it made our eyes water. The bags of potatoes weighed 50 pounds each so we couldn't carry them; we had to drag them across the floor to the door. Not only did the sacks stink, they also oozed rotten potato juice, and soon the floor was slippery with the yucky smelling stuff.

"Whoa, I think I'm gonna puke," Dewey announced. "C'mon Dewey. This should be easy for you. You're used to rank smells," Chick said. We all laughed at Chick.

With the potatoes on the ground, we cut the strings to open the bags, then dumped the potatoes into the first tank, water and rotten potato juice splattering all over. When the tank was almost full, Dougie and I began sorting through the smelly mess, tossing good potatoes into the second tank. Dewey and Chick swished the potatoes around in that tank and then tossed them into the third tank. If one of us would get ahead, he would go to the third tank, fish out the good potatoes, and put them in clean burlap bags. These were stored against the back wall of the store for drying.

The first tank was soon filled with pungent smelling water

and tons of rotten potatoes. Then we had to take a big shovel and scoop the potatoes out of the water and into the back of the pickup truck. We tipped the tank to empty it and then filled it with fresh water. The smell intensified as we worked, attracting every fly within five miles.

After several hours, our boss told us to take a break. He went into the store and returned with a bottle of pop for each of us. We sat in the shade behind the truck and sipped our pop. "This has to be the worst job in the world," Chick commented.

"It probably stinks more than any other job," Dougie said. "Yeah, except for working on the rendering truck," I said.

"Oh yeah, the gut wagon. That has to be pretty bad, too." Dewey said.

We laughed at the thought of the gut wagon, figuring that it would be worse to work with dead cows than with rotten potatoes. "Well, boys, time to get back at it," our boss said.

We had about a third of the potatoes unloaded and washed by noon. We were covered with potato juice, dirt, and mud, and not smelling good ourselves. The noon siren blew and our boss told us to take an hour off for lunch. "You guys wanna come over and have lunch at my place?" Dougie said. "My mom has hotdogs and we could grill out." That sounded like a great idea so off we went to Dougie's. Chick and Dewey got the charcoal out of Dougie's garage and they were going to light the grill while Dougie and I got the hotdogs and stuff from indoors. His mom was upstairs when we walked in. "Hey, Mom! The guys and I are gonna barbeque hotdogs for lunch, okay?"

"Sure, I'll be right down to help you," her voice trailed down from the bedroom.

We were gathering up chips, cookies, and ketchup when Dougie's mom came down the stairs. "Good God! What's that terrible smell?" she asked.

Dougie and I looked at each other.

"I don't smell anything, Mom," he said. "Me, either," I said.

She sniffed the air as she came closer to us. "My goodness,

you two stink. What are you covered with?" We looked at each other and saw the dried potato juice and dirt.

"Well, it might be rotten potato juice," Dougie said, sheepishly.

"You guys get outside. You'll stink up the whole house. I'll bring the stuff out to you," she said, shooing us out the door.

Dewey and Chick had the fire going and we were soon cremating wieners and stuffing chips and cookies into our mouths until there wasn't a scrap of food left. "Yummy! That was good. Now, for a little nap, and I'll be ready to work again." Dewey said. We had about a half hour to snooze, so we stretched out in the shade. It seemed like just a few seconds until Dougie's mom came out of the house.

"You guys are late for work. Someone called from the store to ask about you," she announced. We jumped on our bikes and rode like the wind to the store. This time it didn't seem like the smell was so bad. Guess we had become accustomed to it.

The truck was about half unloaded. Chick and Dewey climbed into the trailer and began dragging sacks of potatoes to the door to dump them. It wasn't long until Dewey appeared at the door. "C'mere, guys, Chick's stuck."

Dougie and I climbed into the truck and walked to Dewey who was peering over the pile of potatoes.

"Where's Chick?" I questioned.

"I'm down here," Chick said, from behind the pile of potatoes.

"Where?" echoed Dougie. "Down here," hollered Chick.

I saw his hand projecting from the pile of potatoes. "How did you get down there?" Dougie inquired.

"I crawled on top of the pile to see how far we had to go yet and I sank between the bags of potatoes. I can't get out!"

Dougie and I crawled up and saw Chick's head sticking up out of the pile.

"Hi, Chick. What are you doing in such a nasty place?" Dougie said, laughing.

"Real funny. Get me out of here. I can barely breathe," he

175

gagged.

Dougie and I began pulling bags of potatoes to the edge and Dewey dragged them to the back of the truck. It took some time to reach Chick. Every time he moved, he went deeper into the potatoes. Finally, his elbows and arms were free, and by pulling, and him pushing, we freed him.

"Are you okay?" I asked.

"Yeah, I think so, but I'm sure covered with potato juice, and I've got the world's worst wedgie," Chick said.

Dougie and I started laughing at that, and while we were rolling in laughter, Chick was pulling and tugging on his underwear to get rid of his wedgie.

It was past suppertime when we finally got the last of the potatoes dumped, washed, and bagged. We cleaned up the cow tanks and used the hose to rinse the potato slime off the parking lot. When our boss paid us $20 each, we felt like kings!

"We should celebrate," Dougie said.

"Sure! Let's eat at the A & W tonight," I said. "Yeah, let's," the rest agreed.

"We need to clean up first. Let's meet there in a half hour," Dougie said. We headed home.

My mom just about fainted when I walked in. "Get out of here. You smell like a sewer," she barked.

"But Mom, I gotta clean up. We are going to eat at the A & W tonight," I argued.

"You're not coming in this house smelling like that. Take soap and a towel, and clean clothes, and go to your beloved Gosey to take your bath," she commanded. That was fine with me. Mom got everything ready for me while I waited outside. "Leave your stinky clothes in the yard when you come home. I'll find a way to clean them," she ordered.

I was as happy as a lark as I rode to the Gosey. When I got there, Dougie was already in the water with a bar of soap. "Your mom didn't like your smell?" I laughed.

"No kidding! She kicked me out of the house," he pouted. I

176

stripped off my rotten-smelling clothes and jumped in the water. A minute later, Chick appeared with clean clothes, a towel, and soap.

"Ah, the communal bath," he laughed, as he stripped off clothes and waded in. "I wonder if Dewey's mom let him clean up at home?" I said. Just then, Dewey's bike rattled up.

"Hey guys, you bathing here, too?" We laughed and splashed and had a great time in the Gosey. Soon we loaded up our stuff and headed to the A & W.

We sat at one of the picnic tables under the awning and a carhop, a high school girl, came bouncing up to take our order. "Hi, guys. What would you like to eat tonight?" she asked, with a sweet grin. We were all agog when a pretty girl treated us nicely so we giggled and laughed but managed to come up with our order. She delivered our food and we devoured our meal, enjoying our time together. We paid up and left her a nice tip. It was a good thing to be rich.

"Well, what should we do now?" Dewey asked.

"Something restful. We worked hard today," Chick said. "Let's go to the Gosey and watch fireflies," Dougie suggested. "Good idea," I said.

We rode to the Gosey and sat on the bank. It was dusk and soon we saw the first flicker of fireflies in the shadows. We sat there talking and laughing, with our bellies full, and our backs tired. All was well.

Hobos

I lived near the west edge of town. There were houses on the other side of my street and then the woods began. My street was blacktopped, but the roads that ran off into the woods were gravel. The sleighing hill was two blocks from my house and across the street from that, in the woods, lived a couple of hobos. Now, they weren't really hobos, in the true sense. Hobos rode trains from place to place and lived off the land and from handouts. These old guys stayed put and didn't ride trains. There were three of them. Each had a little shack made of scrap lumber, tin, and tar paper. The shanties were about ten feet square and rickety, but they seemed to be good enough to make the old guys comfortable. They walked to town every day for their daily visit and to shop for a bottle of cheap wine at the liquor store. Then they ambled back to their little shanties.

Of course, our moms told us to stay clear of them because they were drinkers and weren't a good influence on thirteen year-old boys. Our only contact with them was when they walked past my house. Occasionally Chick, Dougie, Dewey, and I would sneak down to their shanty town to sort through their pile of empty bottles, looking for returnable bottles that we could sell.

One of the old guys was called Bonnie. We wondered why he had a girl's name, but we never found out. He was a hard-looking man who always scowled and growled at us if we passed him on the street. He would often sit on a bench in front of one of the taverns with the other guys and chat the day away, chewing tobacco, and spitting on the sidewalk. The men would take a strip of inner tube from their pockets to snap at flies that came to feast on the spit. Some of them would talk to us as we walked by and tell us stories, but not Bonnie. He never talked and always looked like he was mad about something. We stayed away from him.

Another old guy was Lou. He had a droopy face. The left side of his face looked like it was partly melted. He was nice enough, but scary looking. He always talked to us.

The last old guy was Fungy. He was skinny and had a sad face and a big hump on his back. He didn't say much but he seemed friendly. The kids in town made fun of him as he walked back and forth from his shanty.

One day Dougie and I were riding our bikes uptown when we met Fungy. We pulled our bikes off the sidewalk so he could pass, and he thanked us.

"No problem, Sir," Dougie said.

Fungy stopped and looked at us. I'm sure no one had called him "sir" in a long time. His face looked kindly and he smiled and tipped his hat. We didn't think we had done anything outstanding. We got on our bikes and continued. Fungy was carrying a sack of groceries and continued towards his shanty.

We rode to Chick's house and found him painting the trim on his mom's porch. "Hey guys, I have more brushes," Chick said, cheerfully.

I looked at Dougie and we shook our heads in opposition.

"Sorry, we got something real important to do," I said. Chick began to whine but we didn't even stay to listen. Painting was not one of our favorites.

"Let's go back to my house and see what mom's got to eat," I said.

We set off and as we turned the corner, Dougie said, "Hey! What's in the street?" We checked and found a package of hot dogs.

"Where do you suppose they came from?" I said, as I picked them up.

"I'll bet Fungy dropped them," Dougie said. "He was carrying groceries."

"We should give them back to him," I said.

Dougie agreed so we rode off towards the woods. We stopped near the shanties. "Which one is his?" Dougie asked.

"I don't know," I shrugged.

"Well, I hate to just start knocking on doors. What if we meet Bonnie?" Dougie was worried about the same thing.

We didn't know what to do but we finally walked up to one of the shanties. This was a strange place. The huts were set about twenty feet apart and there were piles of bottles here and there and a place for an outdoor fire. Junk was scattered around and it looked spooky in the dim light of the woods.

"Are you boys lost?" A voice came from one of the shanties, and Dougie and I almost jumped out of our tennis shoes.

"No, we found a package of hot dogs on the street and we thought someone from here might have dropped them," I said.

The door of the middle shanty opened and Fungy walked out, all drooped over. "I was wondering about them," he said, laughing. "I thought I was losing my mind, just dreaming that I had bought them." We laughed, too, and handed over the hot dogs.

"Here," Dougie said.

"We figured they were yours since you had a grocery bag with you earlier," we added.

"That was mighty kind of you to return them," Fungy said. "Would you boys like a cold pop?" Dougie and I looked at each other. "Sure," we said.

Fungy went into his shanty and came out with two bottles of Coke and an opener. "Don't look so shocked," he said. "I don't drink wine all the time. I like a Coke once in a while, too." We laughed and he motioned for us to sit down on the bench by the shack.

"So, you guys like to fish?" he asked.

"Yeah, we do. How d'you know?" I said.

"You've usually got poles and tackle in your bike baskets. I just figured that means you fish," Fungy laughed.

"Do you fish, Mr. Uh?" Dougie asked.

Fungy smiled. "My name is Faye, not Fungy, like you kids call me. Yeah, I fish. I used to fish a lot more till my back got so bad."

Dougie and I looked at each other. Wow! The guy fished.

"I enjoyed fishing for northerns," Faye said. "I've caught some good ones in my day, too." He looked like he was remembering long ago fishing trips.

"How did ... , I mean, what happened to your back?" I said, "...if you don't mind telling us."

"It's a spinal disease," he said. "It started when I was in the army and it kept getting worse; got so bad that I couldn't work and, well, this is where I ended up."

"You don't have a family?" Dougie asked.

"No one living, anymore," Faye said. "I get a small pension from the army that is just enough to keep me going."

Dougie and I were surprised to learn these things about Faye and also to realize that he was just an ordinary guy, similar to others, except that he had come into bad luck. We sat and talked to Faye for most of the afternoon and he told us about the army and we had a great time together. We told him about our big bass catch earlier in the summer.

"Yeah, I saw your picture in the paper," he said. "Those were some nice ones."

It was about suppertime so Dougie and I said goodbye and told Faye that we were happy that we got to know him. He told us to come back, anytime.

"Gosh, he's a nice man," Dougie said, as we headed home.

"You know, I think we should try to give him a hand; maybe help him with chores, or take him food once in a while," I said.

Dougie agreed and we both felt fortunate that we had made a new friend.

The next day the four of us were at the Gosey and we told Chick and Dewey about Faye.

"I always thought he was just a creepy guy that we should stay away from," Dewey confided.

"He's just like someone's grandpa," I said.

"If you don't look at the hump on his back, he's just a great old guy; friendly, and not a monster," Dougie elaborated.

That day we caught several catfish and a couple of bass. We decided to clean them and take a few fillets to Faye. The four of us rode to the shanties and we walked up to Faye's. I knocked on the door. He smiled from ear to ear when he saw us.

"Faye, this is Dewey and Chick. We were fishing today and got a lot of fish, so we thought you might like some for your supper," I said.

"Thanks boys. That would be great," he said, as we handed him the fish. "Could I get you a Coke, or something?"

"No, thanks," we said. "We gotta get home for supper. Maybe next time."

He thanked us again and we biked back.

"You were right," Chick said. "He's no monster."

From then on, we kept a sharp watch for stuff for Faye. We'd take him tomatoes from the garden if we had extras and carrots and potatoes as we dug them. We took him cleaned fish and managed to sneak homemade cookies and bread when we could pilfer it without getting caught. When we saw him on the street, we rode along with him and chatted and called him Faye, not Fungy. We told him about the Gosey and how we spent so much time there. He said that he swam in the Gosey when he was a kid. One day when we were fishing, Faye appeared with his fishing pole and he fished with us all afternoon. We took a swim later but he wouldn't go in the water, even though we pestered him for a half hour. He had fun just talking with us and fishing.

Sometimes we would take Cokes and chips to Faye's and sit in the shade and listen to his stories about the army and going to war, and all the other things he had done in his life. We took our own pop so we wouldn't consume his Cokes. If we took ice cream cones, we had to ride fast so his wouldn't melt. He always was happy to see us and we were happy to keep company with him.

Then one day we were headed to Faye's with half an apple pie and homemade cookies. We noticed Mr. Audetta's police car parked in the street by the shanties. We walked down the path to the shack. "What are you boys doing here?" Mr. Audetta asked.

"We came to see Faye. He's our friend. We brought pie and cookies for him," Dewey said.

A sad look came over Mr. Audetta's face. "I might have known," he said. "You guys were the friends he was talking about when he passed on."

We stood there, stunned. "Passed on?" Dougie said.

"Bonnie got me early this morning. Faye was very sick and they thought he should go to the hospital," Mr. Audetta said. "I checked and found him indeed very ill so I radioed for the ambulance. Before it got here, he was gone." The four of us just stood there staring. I could feel my eyes welling with tears but I didn't want the other guys to see. I looked away and saw the others doing the same thing.

Mr. Audetta came over and put his arms on our shoulders.

"Just before he died, Faye asked me to tell you how much he appreciated your kindness," he said. "I didn't know who he was talking about, but now, I do. Do you know how much he enjoyed your visits? You did a good thing, and made an old man very happy, right up to the minute he died."

The guys and I were speechless. We were holding sadness in and tears back and there wasn't a thing we could say that wouldn't have opened the floodgate, so we nodded our heads and walked back to our bikes. We rode to the Gosey and sat in the sand by the swimming hole. We dug our toes into the sand and stared at the river. Faye was the first person we knew well who had died. It was a new experience; one that was very hard to understand.

They buried Faye a few days later and gave him a military funeral, with a firing squad, taps, and all. They placed a flag over his casket. Bonnie, Lou, Mr. Audetta, and the four of us attended, along with other VFW guys with the firing squad, and a high school kid who played taps. It was a small funeral. When they shot the guns and played taps, we had tears streaming down our cheeks. After they buried Faye, we rode our bikes to the Gosey and sat for a long time, watching the river run, and thinking of our friend.

"He's probably fishin' in heaven," Dougie said.

"Yeah, catching huge northerns," I said, "standing straight and tall."

Big Shots

The town doctor lived across the alley from my house. His office was in the lower part of a big house and he lived upstairs. It was convenient for my family because, with three boys, there was always someone with an injury, and Dr. Klockow was great about letting us in the back door for a quick treatment. I always thought he worked too much. It seemed odd to me that he never took time off for fishing. He would go duck and pheasant hunting in the fall. Otherwise, he just worked.

He loved cars. He always had a brand new one in his driveway behind the office because every year, like clockwork, he traded cars before the old one was even broken in. I guess he could afford to do so. He also liked vintage cars. One day, while Dougie and I were feeding my critters, a flatbed trailer loaded with an old black Ford Model A pulled into the alley. Dr. Klockow came out, excited about the car, and instructed the men to put it in a shed behind his office.

"Whatcha gonna do with that old car, Doc?" I asked. "Someday I'm going to fix it up and take it for a Sunday drive," he said.

Dougie and I thought it was foolish to have a car just to drive on Sunday, but it was his money.

The car sat in the shed for many weeks and Doc, and everyone else, seemed to forget about it. But one day Dougie and I decided to get a closer look. We admitted ourselves to the shed. The outside of the car was covered with dust but inside it was clean and nice. The seats were red velvet and the side windows had little window shades. It was a four-door. The front seats had velvet backs with flower vases built into the ends. It was fancy, alright! We had thought that maybe Doc would fix it up, and then when we got old enough to drive, he would let us use it for a fishing car, but fishing cars don't have flower vases.

The next day we took Chick and Dewey to the shed to show

them the car. They were admiring it and Chick suggested we see how it would be to sit in. We got in, Chick was behind the wheel, and Dougie was in the front seat with him. Dewey and I climbed in the back. We pretended that we were cruising around, waving at imaginary people, and just having a great time. We were careful not to damage anything in the few hours we fooled around.

A couple of days later, we were getting ready for a baseball game, but we had time to kill. "Hey, guys! Let's go for a drive in the old car," Dewey said. We jumped up and before long we were sitting in the car. It was Dougie's turn to drive and he shifted gears and off we went to imaginary destinations.

"Hey, guys! Look what I got from my brother!" Dewey said, producing a can of Copenhagen snuff. We looked at the little round box. "It's chew," he said. "You put a little inside your lip and it tastes good."

"Have you ever done it?" I asked.

"Not yet, but I thought it would be a good thing for a road trip," Dewey said.

None of us had ever tried chew but we had seen the old guys in town using it.

"Here," Dewey said, opening the box and holding a pinch out to me. I looked at Chick and Dougie and they nodded yes, so I took some between my first finger and thumb. "Now put it between your lower lip and teeth," Dewey said. He took a pinch and demonstrated.

Dewey passed the chew to Dougie and Chick and we all put it in our mouths at once. There was silence in the car as we got the first taste of the chew. It was hard to describe; a mint taste mixed with licorice, or something that had a strong taste. I looked at the others as they were getting their first impression, trying to figure out if they liked it or not.

"Good stuff, eh?" Dewey exclaimed.

"Yeah, good," Dougie answered.

"Yup," Chick agreed.

I just nodded. Soon my mouth began to fill with saliva.

"What do you do with all the juice?" I asked.

"Just swallow it. That's the best part," Dewey said. We nodded in agreement as if we were old hands at chewing and we began to swallow the juice. Dougie was driving and we waved at pretend people as we swallowed chew juice. Pretty soon Chick rolled down his window.

"Whew, it's getting hot in here." "No kidding," I said. "Hot as heck."

I had swallowed enough of the chew juice that my stomach felt like it had a rock in it and four or five flopping fish slapping their tails on the rock. My head was throbbing as if it could fall off my shoulders, my eyes were watering, and my ears were ringing. I looked at Dewey and he was as green as the Incredible Hulk.

"Dewey, you don't look so good," I said.

"I'm feeling pretty yucky," Dewey admitted, and he grabbed the door handle and fell to the dirt floor and threw up.

That started a chain reaction. I stuck my head out the window and blew up, too. When Dougie saw that he did the same-out the front window. Chick managed to get his door open but didn't get far enough away from Dewey and threw up all over Dewey's tennis shoes.

We got out of the car and staggered into the daylight. Dewey stopped and blew up again and so did Dougie. Chick and I both made it to the back of my chicken house before round two. The four of us weaved back and forth to the shade of our big maple tree where we stretched out on the grass, thankful for the cool breeze.

"Oh, my gosh! I think I'm gonna die," Dewey wailed.

"Great idea you had there, Dewey," Dougie said.

"Yeah! Thanks for the chew, Dewey," I added.

Chick was too weak to talk, so he just punched Dewey in the leg.

We stayed there, listening to the birds and the soothing

sound of the wind, and soon we began to feel better. "What do you think, guys? Baseball time?" I asked. Everyone sat up and decided things were okay.

"Dewey, you know where you can put that chew, don't you?" Chick asked.

"Don't worry. It's going in the trash," Dewey said. "I'm not going to show you what else I had." Of course, that heightened our interest.

"What, Dewey?" Dougie asked.

"Forget it. You'll get mad at me," Dewey said. He walked to our trashcan and threw the chew can in and then reached in his other pocket and withdrew half a pack of cigarettes. He tossed them in, too. "I think we can have fun without these," he jabbered.

We played baseball that day and continued to visit the old car for many months until one day a man came with a flatbed trailer and hauled it away. Doc never told us what happened to it. It had been a fun place to imagine adventures and it had been the place where we became introduced to chewing tobacco. The imagining had been great fun but the chew was something we never tried again. We weren't stupid. We had learned our lesson.

Mad As Hornets

The four of us were fishing above the bridge just downstream from the Gosey. Now that we were experienced river fishermen, we often fished near the bridge by the pier. The pier was left over from an old toll bridge that had been torn down long before our time. The rock pillars of the old bridge had once crossed the entire river but now most of them had been washed away by the current and ice. The one we called Snake Island-because snakes liked it there-remained. It was about fifteen feet from the shore, about twenty feet across and ten feet high.

Snake Island caused a break in the river current, creating an eddy. Fish pooled in the slack water and that was why we often fished there.

We generally used a hook, sinker, and worm and fished on the bottom, watching the tip of our pole for a bite. Sometimes we used spinners and lures, but because of their expense, we saved them for special occasions.

We were having good luck and fun-fishing, telling stories, and being teenage boys-when a man arrived on the scene and started fishing by Snake Island. He caught our attention because he looked like he had stepped off the cover of an L.L. Bean catalog. He was wearing tan chest waders, a tan shirt with those flaps

on the shoulders that made you look like you were in the army, a tan vest with about ten thousand little pockets, and a tan hat that looked like the one Sherlock Holmes wore. He was carrying a fly rod that probably cost more than all our gear put together, and that included our bikes.

"Who's that? Doctor Livingston, I presume?" Dewey said, rather loudly, and the guy looked at us.

"Shh, Dewey! That's Mr. Doctor Livingston to you," Chick laughed. We cracked up. The man continued to fish and soon he had a huge smallmouth bass making a splash behind his popping bug. He jerked back but missed the fish.

"Wow, did you see that bass?" Dougie asked. "It was huge. I hope he doesn't catch it."

We all agreed that it would be unfortunate to see a stranger catch a big bass from our river. Then the bass grabbed at his popper again. He missed it a second time. We snickered and made ourselves obnoxious. The bass smashed his popper a third time. He missed it again and this time his popper flew into the air and landed in a treetop on the bank above him. He set off up the bank to retrieve his popper. We were rolling in the sand, laughing.

I reeled in and ran up the bank to where the man had been.

I laid my pole in the grass and went in search of a frog. I spotted one and hooked him through the lips and tossed him into the current above Snake Island. As the frog made his way back to the bank, the bass grabbed him. I let the line go and waited a few seconds and then I set the hook. The bass headed upstream, jumped up out of the water, turned downstream, jumped again, and headed back toward the middle of the river. I fought the big fish like a professional and soon had him on his side next to the bank.

By that time the rest of the guys were cheering me on and when the bass came close to the bank, Dougie reached down and picked it up by the lower jaw.

"That's a good one," Chick said.

"Not bad," Dewey broke in.

The L.L. Bean guy was standing with his mouth hanging open and when Dougie held the bass up for him to see, he gave a jerk on his line, broke off his popper, and walked away. We just about split, we laughed so hard.

"Dear Chap, shall I release this little one, or will you have your picture taken with it for the cover of the next catalog?" Dougie mimicked. We roared with laughter at that, too.

"Put the little fellow back," I said, "It's not worth a photo."

Dougie opened the fish's mouth and removed the hook. The frog was still hooked and although very much alive, he was probably scared to death.

Dougie took the fish and slid it back into the water and carefully unhooked the frog and let it go. It hopped up the bank along the grass until it was out of sight.

"Well, that was fun," I said, with a smirk. "I'll bet that guy never comes back here to fish."

We took up fishing again and as the afternoon wore on, it began to get real hot and humid. You could almost drink the air. Ominous thunderclouds were building in the west. "We should go to Gutweiler's Lake and fish before the rain," Dougie said. "You know how the bass and northerns bite when a storm is coming." We rolled up our lines and headed to Gutweiler's. It wasn't far from town.

We arrived and took our hooks and sinkers off and put on one of our precious northern and bass lures. My favorite and luckiest lure was my red and white *Bass 0 Reno*. Dougie had a *Bass 0 Reno*, too, but his was painted to look like a frog. Chick liked his *Johnson Silver Spoon* best and Dewey used a big *Mepps* spinner.

We cast along the shoreline, working our way down the lake.

"Whew, I'd like to take a swim," Dewey said.

"Yeah, me too. It's way too hot," Chick said.

The storm clouds were still a long way off, so we decided to take a dip to cool off. It didn't take long to get out of our shorts and shirts and soon we were in the water, splashing, and yelling, and having a great time.

"Hey, let's swim to the duck blind on the other side," Dewey said.

"Yeah, let's. I want to see it," Dougie said.

We set off across the lake to the duck blind only about a hundred yards away. It was in shallow water so when we got near it, we were able to walk through the lily pads and mud. It was a fine blind, about eight feet square, with a little place in the back to hide the hunter's boat or canoe. In the fall, it had been covered with grass, but now it was mostly chicken wire with bits of brown grass hanging here and there.

"Let's go in," Dewey said, and he climbed up the ladder into the blind. Chick went next; then Dougie; then me. As I stepped on the floor, Dewey sat down on a bench near the back. When he sat, we heard a humming noise.

"What's that?" Chick cried. Dougie and I listened. "Sounds like bees," I said.

Suddenly Dewey came running at us, screaming. Behind him were about a thousand bees buzzing and stinging and raising one heck of a noise. I was backing down the ladder and Dewey ran into me and the two of us fell into the water outside the blind. It only took about half a second for Dougie and Chick to join us. Once we were in the water, the bees began diving and landing on us, stinging us. We ran through the mud toward the deeper water and the bees followed us. When we got to deeper water, we were able to protect our bodies, but the bees kept going after our heads. We screamed and yelled and swam away as fast as we could.

Finally we had escaped the stinging monsters. We were panting and stopped to catch our breath. We had numerous stings on our faces and heads. Chick had one on his left eyelid and his eye had swollen shut. Dougie had one on his lip that made him look like a boxer that had taken a good one in the mouth. Poor Dewey had about half a dozen stings so his whole face was red and swollen out of shape. I had a couple of good ones on my right ear making it about twice its normal size.

And then the rain started. The wind picked up and we were in the middle of the lake.

"We better get out of here in case there is lightning, and we'll all get cooked," Dougie shouted over the wind. We headed for shore. It was raining so hard we could barely see ten feet in front of us. We gathered up our clothes and fishing gear and trudged back through the woods. The cool rain eased the pain of the stings, so we didn't bother to dress until we got to our bikes. Then we pulled on our drenched clothes. Dewey bent over to put his foot into his shorts and Chick began laughing. There, on Dewey's butt, were two bee stings, one in the middle of each cheek. It looked like two red eyes looking back at us. Dewey could see we were checking him out so he put his hands back to feel. "Well, it looks like I'll be riding my bike standing up," he said. We laughed like crazy and began the muddy trip to town. When we arrived, the rain had subsided and the sun was peeking through in the western sky.

"Looks like the storm is over," announced Dougie.

"Think they are still biting at the bridge?" I wondered aloud.

Dewey, Chick, and Dougie looked at each other and shrugged.

"What the heck, what else do we have to do?" Chick said. We turned toward the river and rode single file back toward the bridge. Dewey was in the lead, standing up.

Harvest Festival

The last big event of the summer was the Harvest Festival. It was like a county fair but on a smaller scale. There was a big parade and there were rides, games, and opportunity for local people to bring exhibits to the public school to be judged. Everything from jam and pies, to cattle and pigs, was awarded ribbons and cash prizes. It was an exciting time for those of us in the animal business, like Dougie and me.

The deadline for entries was fast approaching and Dougie and I were planning to enter several inhabitants of our backyard zoos. Dougie was taking pigeons and rabbits. I would take pigeons, as well as chickens and turtles. The rules stipulated one male and two females of each animal. With chickens it was easy to tell, but pigeons were more difficult, and turtles were downright impossible. I wasn't worried because I didn't think the judges would know the difference, either.

Dougie and I helped each other build little traveling cages for transporting our critters. My turtle cage had a large cake pan in the bottom for sand and water so the turtles could get wet. We spent a day preparing and then came the job of deciding which pigeons and chickens should go. We picked the prettiest ones and made certain they were clean and ready to exhibit. When it came to the turtles, I chose a large one, and two smaller ones, the same size. That way if the judge asked me which was the male, I could tell him it was the big one.

The exhibits had to be delivered on Thursday so we loaded up Dougie's dad's car and he drove us to the high school. The animals' exhibit was set up in the bus garage, so we put our animals with the others in the same class. Pigeons were in one class, while chickens were divided into regular and small birds. Of course, my Bantams were small, so I grouped them with the other little chickens. My chickens looked better than the rest and I was confident of winning. Turtles went with "Other Pets."

There were hamsters, guinea pigs, gerbils, and parakeets in this class, but no other turtles, so I was feeling good about that class, too. Dougie and I had competition with our pigeons and there were many rabbits entered, but Dougie's were, by far, the prettiest and largest. We fed and watered our pets and left the area so the judges could do their job.

We paced and worried like a couple of expectant fathers while the judging was going on. They had closed the bus garage doors and the results would be kept secret until the next morning, so Dougie and I decided to get Dewey and Chick and go for a swim at the Gosey to help pass the time.

The next day the festival opened and all the rides and games and food stands were ready for business. We were waiting for the school gym and bus garage to open so we could find out who won prizes. We were not only excited about winning, we were countting on prize money to spend at the festival. We had saved up our bottle and lawn-mowing money but it wouldn't fund three days of fun, so prize money would be a lifesaver. We had decided to pool our wins and share with Dewey and Chick since they helped us with our animals, and they were our best friends.

Finally, the doors opened and in we went. There were swarms of kids and adults waiting to see the animals. We pushed our way through, running to the end of the garage where our entries were.

"First! I got first on the pigeons!" Dougie yelled at me. "What did I get?" I inquired.

"You got a third," he said.

I ran to the chicken area and there was a blue ribbon on my Bantams! "Dougie, I got a first on my chickens!" I yelled.

Dewey shouted from the "Other Pets" area. "You got a first on those stupid turtles!"

"First? That's great!" I bubbled. Obviously the judges knew quality "Other Pets" when they saw them.

Chick shouted from the rabbit area, "Hey, Dougie, You got a first on the rabbits, too."

It was better than we had hoped. We wanted to place in the top three of any of our entries. First place was worth five dollars; second place paid three dollars; and third place was awarded one dollar. Our four first places and one third place had netted us twenty-one dollars. Dewey was adding in his head. "That's twenty dollars!"

"Twenty-one dollars, Dewey. You forgot the third on pigeons," Chick said.

"Twenty-one dollars! Oh boy! Oh boy!" Dewey marveled. We could hardly believe it. With the money we had saved and this windfall, we were rich beyond belief

We ran to the high school office where the festival officials had a table set up where each winner could identify himself and claim the prize money. We stood in line for about a half hour. "Name, please?" said an old lady.

"Dewey," Dewey said. "But I don't got any critters. These guys do." The lady looked at Dougie and me and we gave our names and she handed us our envelopes of cash.

"Thanks, ma'am," we said, and raced off to count our money.

Dougie had a ten-dollar bill and I had a ten and a one.

"We're rich," Dewey said. "What should we eat first?"

We headed for the cotton candy wagon and we each got a paper tube with a huge, blue sticky cloud of cotton candy. Then we walked around the grounds looking at all the games and rides, deciding what to do next.

"Let's try that ride," Chick said. We got in line and rode the Tilt-a- Whirl. It was a wild ride and we laughed and screamed like girls as we spun and whirled around the track. Then we went on the Bullet. It was a bullet-shaped car on the end of an arm with another car on the other end. It rotated like the hands of a clock, spinning upside down and downside up. It was terrifying, but we all had a great time yelling and shouting at each other while we whirled through space. Then I heard a clinking sound.

"What's that?" I asked Dougie.

He looked around our car and suddenly he shouted. "It's money. It's the change I had in my pocket," he groaned.

Sure enough, I felt my pocket and my change was gone, too.

The ride finally stopped and the ride attendant unlocked our car and we jumped out and began searching in the grass for our money.

"Hey! You guys get out of there. You'll get hit by the ride."

"We lost our money, Mister," I said.

"Out! You can't be in here," came the reply.

Dewey and Chick got out of their car and came over to us.

"Check your pockets," Dougie said. They did and they got a sick look on their faces.

"Money gone?" I asked.

"Every dime," Chick said.

"Me, too," Dewey fumed.

"And that guy won't let us look for it," I said, pointing to the man.

"Well, we'll have to come back later," Chick said. There wasn't anything we could do about it, so we left.

"I'm hungry again," Dewey said. We went to the hot dog stand and bought a one-footer. "These are great!" Dewey said, as he squirted mustard and ketchup and piled on pickles and onions.

"Go easy on that stuff, Dewey, or you'll blow up on the next ride," Chick said. Dewey just grinned as he took a big bite.

We rode and ate all day. Late in the afternoon, Dougie and I went home for rabbit and pigeon food and corn for my chickens. I changed the water in the turtle pen and gave each of them a fish worm. Then it was time to go home. We were exhausted from the riding and eating, and it didn't take long for me to fall asleep.

I don't know what woke me up, but just past midnight, I popped awake. The full moon made a bright square of glimmering light on the wall across from my bed. I was half asleep, looking at it, when I saw a shadow of two heads. That woke me up real fast. The two heads ducked down when they heard me move in my bed. Then, slowly, they reappeared. I slipped out of bed and silently edged to the window, staying low so whoever was outside wouldn't see me. The heads disappeared again, and I raised my head. Slowly, Dewey and Chick's heads came up again. Just as they got into view, I said, "Boo!"

"Holy Jeez!" Chick said, and took off running.

Dewey fell over backwards and crawled away as fast as he could.

"What are you guys doing?" I said in an audible whisper.

Chick stopped running. "Holy crap! You almost gave me a heart attack."

"What are you two idiots doing?" I asked, again.

"We're gonna see if we can find the money we lost on the Bullet," Dewey said. "Chick is staying at my house for the night and we decided we should try to get our money back."

"Wanna come along?" Chick said.

"You got flashlights?" I asked. Chick held up three flashlights. "Wait there and be quiet. I'll sneak out." I slipped on my T-shirt and shorts. I went to the back door and picked up my tennis shoes, quietly opened the door, and stepped outside. I slid into my shoes and met the guys behind the house. "What about Dougie?" I said.

"His bedroom is on the second floor. How can we wake him?" Chick said. I didn't have an answer for that, so we walked to Dougie's house and stood in the yard below his bedroom.

"If we try to wake him up, we'll probably wake up everyone in the house," I said. "Let's find the money, and we'll clue him in tomorrow." That seemed like the best plan.

We walked the back streets to the festival grounds and climbed over the railing by the Bullet. It didn't take long to locate the coins in the grass. We picked up many coins. Actually, we found more money than we lost. We had it pretty well cleaned up and decided to check around the other rides. We found a few pennies but when we looked in the grass by the ticket booths, we found dimes and a couple of quarters.

"It's two o'clock. We'd better head home," Dewey said. "Here, you guys. Take these coins and put them with yours.

We can count money in the morning," I said, as I handed the coins to Chick. We walked past Dougie's and then I went off to my house, and Dewey and Chick went back to Dewey's.

Mom came to wake me up at ten o'clock. "Dougie's on the phone. He says you're late and to hurry up," she said.

"Tell him I'll be there in two minutes," I said, as I ran to the bathroom to wash my face and brush my teeth. I threw on my shorts and T-shirt and grabbed my tennis shoes as I went out the door. Dewey and Chick were at Dougie's waiting for me.

"The guys tell me you had an adventure last night," Dougie said.

"Yeah, we couldn't figure out a way to wake you or we would have had you come with us," I said.

"How much did we get, Dewey?" He and Chick got smug looks on their faces.

"Well, thanks to our brilliant plan, we not only found our money. We ended up with about twice as much. We picked up seven dollars and ten cents," Dewey boasted.

"Seven dollars! No way!" Dougie said. Dewey dug into his pocket and pulled out a handful of change.

"Wow! We're rich again!" asserted Dewey.

We still had almost ten dollars remaining from our winnings.

With this new money, it was like starting over, and we hadn't spent a dime of our savings. "This is great. We've got enough money for lots of stuff and if we can sneak out again tonight, we'll have even more," Chick said. Indeed we were riding high. We went to the festival and had a grand day: riding, eating, and acting like thirteen-year-old boys. That night we decided to sleep in the tent to make it easier to go scouting for money. We got up at midnight and made our way to the festival grounds and found almost four dollars. Apparently people were becoming more careful with their change, or they were running out of money.

The parade was on the last day of the festival. It was a grand affair with bands and floats, and fire trucks and noise. We watched from the curb and yelled and clapped at all the wonderful things that passed. We had one last afternoon at the festival. As the day came to an end, we went home and got our bikes and headed to the Gosey. We hadn't been swimming for three days and somehow we just needed to get into the river to relax. It had been a great three days.

We were basking in the water, talking about our good fortune with the animals and finding the lost money and how great the parade was.

"You know, guys," Dougie said, "there's only one week till school starts."

As much as we hated to think about it, Dougie was right. "We have to do something special to end the summer," Chick said.

"Good idea. What can we do?" I asked.

We thought for a while and suddenly Dougie said, "How about a canoe trip down the river?"

"Where are we gonna get canoes?" Dewey said.

"My dad's got one in the garage," Dougie said.

"We can find another one if we think about it," Chick chimed.

"My brother has one. He doesn't live here, but if I call him, I bet he'd let us use it," Dewey offered.

"Okay, that's it. A big end-of-summer trip! Everyone in?" Chick said.

Of course, *All fir one, and one fir all*, we cheered.

Last Hurrah

It was the last week of summer vacation. By Monday, we would be back in the classroom. We had come up with a plan for a canoe trip down the river to spend our last days of freedom in fishing, swimming, and having fun.

Although the idea was hatched on the previous weekend, it took us several days to get permission from our parents and the rest of the week to make the preparations.

On the last Monday of our freedom, we started in. "Oh, c'mon, Mom! We know how to swim, and we know the river."

"How do you know so much about the river? I thought you spent all your time at the Gosey," our mothers replied.

"Well, we, uh; we just know. We are good swimmers and we'll be careful," was our answer.

"I need to check with the other parents to see what they think and then I'll decide," was the response.

I rode to Dougie's, and we called Chick and Dewey. We compared notes, and we knew how our parents were thinking.

"My mom is giving in," Chick said. "I think if she talks to your mom, she'll agree. How about your parents, Dewey?"

"They said okay if you guys are going. They must trust you," he said, smiling.

"Of course, they trust us, Dewey," Dougie said. "We're angels."

After a half dozen phone calls, the adults finally agreed. We began to gather equipment and to figure out how to get our gear to the river. Dougie's dad gave us use of his canoe, and Dewey's brother was willing also to give us his, but he couldn't deliver it until Wednesday. That meant we couldn't leave until Thursday morning. We had two days to round up all the supplies for our four-day trip.

We decided to use Chick's tent because of its size and its ease in setting up. Our camping stuff was handy because we had used it all summer. We rounded up an ax, a small saw, and several coolers for the food. Dewey's brother was bringing us a jug for fresh water.

Then we dug enough worms for four days of fishing. Our worm-digging place was almost depleted because we had been harvesting worms all summer and the ones we had been finding were puny. But we dug and dug and managed to find a supply for the trip.

Since we had been so fortunate at the Harvest Festival, our finances were in good shape. Between us, we had over twenty dollars. We went to Mr. Kalsher's grocery store and carefully checked prices on the things we needed, such as eggs--two each for four days came to thirty-two so we got three dozen. Then we got three pounds of bacon, three pounds of butter, a bag of flour, and two bottles of oil for frying fish. We picked up two bags of potatoes and four large cans of beans. With the addition of four loaves of bread and four packages of ham and bologna, we were set with the essentials. We checked our cash and found that we had enough for Jiffy Pops popcorn, marshmallows, twelve packs of Kool-Aid, and an assortment of candy and chips. We ended up spending every penny we had.

Our moms made us sleep at home the night before our trip. I could barely close my eyes and I slept very little, waiting eagerly for the morning. Finally at six-thirty, I got up and packed my duffle bag with clothes and soap and my toothbrush. Mom made breakfast and hugged me goodbye like she wasn't ever going to see me again.

"Be a good boy, and don't do anything stupid," she called, as I flew out the door.

"Bye, Mom. See you Sunday," I echoed.

We gathered at Chick's house since he lived close to the river.

The gear was sitting in his garage and we began hauling it to the river. It took four trips each and an hour for us to cart everything to the water's edge. His mom came to see us off "Are you sure you have everything?"

"Yes, Mom," Chick said.

"Yes, Mom," the rest of us said.

His mom laughed. "You nuts be careful."

"There are whirlpools in the river that will suck you to the bottom and drown you," we chorused.

She shook her head and walked up on the riverbank. "Have fun. Remember Dougie's dad will pick you up at the last bridge before the Mississippi. For God's sake, don't go paddling out into the Mississippi or we'll never see you again."

"Sure, Mom," we promised.

Dougie and Chick were in one canoe and Dewey and I in the other. Dougie and I shoved the canoes into the water and jumped in. We paddled into the current and slipped down the river toward the bridge. We turned and waved to Chick's mom on the bank. We were off on our great adventure.

We paddled for about a half hour. We wanted to get far away from home so no one could change their mind and spoil our trip. If we got away fast, we would be safe. We were a couple of miles from home when Dewey decided we should stop for lunch.

"Dewey, it's only ten o'clock in the morning. We just had breakfast," we protested.

"Yeah, but we're on vacation, and we don't have any place to go and no special time to be there. So, let's take it easy and have fun," Dewey said.

For once, Dewey was right. We had no schedule, no parents to set a curfew, or tell us when to eat, no teachers to correct us, and nothing to do but have fun.

"Dewey's right," Chick said. "Let's stop to fish and eat." It made sense so we looked for a sandbar with a nice drop off "I'll make sandwiches," Dewey offered.

"I'll cut pole holders," Dougie said.

"I'll unload the fishing poles and bait," Chick said.

"I'll gather firewood and make the campfire," I said.

In a short time we were sitting comfortably in the sand, feasting on bologna sandwiches and chips, and drinking grape Kool-Aid. After eating, we went to the edge of the sandbar, dangled our feet in the water, and fished.

It was sunny and warm so we peeled off our shirts, rolling over on our sides as we watched for bites, talking and laughing, just like we did at the Gosey. Dewey soon had a catfish and Chick, a bass. Then Dougie and I each had a catfish.

"This is a good fishing hole. Maybe we should stay here for the rest of the day and camp here tonight," I said. Everyone agreed, so we settled in for our first day on the river.

It was a great day. Our stringer was filled with fish so we decided to swim. We stripped off our shorts, splashed, yelled, and made a huge sand castle in the damp sand. Too soon, the sun slipped beneath the trees.

"Looks like we better set up the tent and make supper," Dougie said.

"I'll help Dewey with the fish, and you two work on the tent," I suggested. Dewey and I cleaned the fish and washed the fillets in the river. Then we stoked up the fire and placed the metal grate over it for frying the fish. Dewey was the chef and I helped him prepare the potatoes and onions. We had flour, spices, and oil for frying the fillets. I opened a can of beans and placed it on the grate and soon the sandbar area began to smell real good. Dougie and Chick came out of the tent, sniffing like a couple of coon dogs.

"Jeez! That smells good, Dewey," Chick said.

"Of course! I'm a fine chef," Dewey gloated, grinning from ear to ear.

After a few minutes, the fish and potatoes were ready, so we each took a serving while Dewey continued to fry fish. We ate and ate until we groaned, patting our full bellies. Every scrap of fish, potatoes, and beans was gone along with almost a loaf of bread.

"I think I died and went to heaven," Chick said. We laughed and kicked back to rest. We were planning the next day and anticipating the new adventures when we started to yawn.

"What d'ya think, guys?" I asked.

"I think it's time for bed," Dewey sighed.

"Yup," was one answer.

"Yeah! Me, too," came another.

"Then it's unanimous," I said.

"Unanimous? Yeah, unanimous here, too," Dougie said.

We laughed and, one by one, we wiped off our sandy feet, stripped to our underwear and climbed into our sleeping bags. We listened to the marsh sounds from across the narrow channel. There were frogs croaking, crickets singing, and an occasional hoot of an owl. It was so cool. Soon Dewey was snoring and then Chick.

"You awake, Dougie?" I whispered. "Yeah."

"This is pretty cool, huh?"

"Yeah, very cool. Night," he faded off

"Night."

I was partly awake and my mind was trying to figure out where I was when I heard Dewey roll over and fart. Soon the tent was filled with that all too-familiar smell and it roused us at once. Then, the comments of disgust: Holy cow, jeez, etc.

Chick, Dougie, and I were attempting to evacuate the tent at the same time and we almost knocked it down. Dewey was still sleeping. We escaped into the fresh morning air and dressed.

"Dewey, you stink. Go to the marsh and bury yourself," Chick yelled into the tent. Dewey rolled onto his stomach and let another one fly. We shrieked with laughter, and soon Dewey was laughing so hard, he shook the tent.

"C'mon, get up and fix us breakfast, Chef Dewey Boy R Dee," Dougie said.

We had eggs and bacon, burnt bread, and green Kool-Aid for breakfast. We seemed to lack the technique for toasting bread over an open fire, so it turned to charcoal, but we ate it anyway. We cleaned the pans, packed up our junk, and loaded the canoes. We were careful not to leave any garbage and to extinguish the fire, and we said goodbye to our first campsite.

We paddled along, not in a hurry, but not poking along, either, and soon we had passed under the bridges of the two towns downriver from us. From there, the river meandered through wooded and swampy areas, but passed no towns. We pulled up on a sandbar for lunch and then continued our trip downstream. By this time, it had become hot and we looked for a place to take a swim and then a nap. We dozed and suddenly I woke up and realized that much of the day had been spent. "Hey, guys! Wake up. We slept the afternoon away," I muttered. The guys woke up, one by one, and yawned, and stretched.

"Cripes, we slept a long time," Dougie exclaimed.

"Well, this would be a good place to spend the night," Chick suggested. "Let's make supper."

We baited up and soon we had fish for our supper. "Same thing as last night?" I asked.

"That worked for me," Dougie said. He and Chick were on the tent and wood detail and Dewey and I cleaned fish and began supper. We were getting good at this, and it wasn't long before the smell of fried potatoes with onions and fresh fish filled the air. I put a can of beans on, despite the effect they had on Dewey. After we finished eating, we stretched back in the warm sand and began our usual conversation. It didn't amount to much; just the same old stuff we talked about whenever we laid around; the stuff that made us laugh and feel good.

Because of the long afternoon nap, we were totally awake and stayed up late. Dewey decided he wanted popcorn so he got a Jiffy Pop and laid it on the fire grate.

"Don't get that too hot, Dewey, or it will burn," I instructed. "Who's the chef here?" Dewey inquired. "You gotta get it hot. Then it pops fast."

"Okay, Dewey. You know best, but don't forget there's one Jiffy Pop for each of us."

Dewey's Jiffy Pop began to sizzle, and then the corn started popping, and then ... black smoke.

"Oh, boy! Time to shake it," Dewey said, grabbing the wire handle. The handle was scorching hot and he dropped it on the grate. He grabbed his T-shirt to use as a pot holder, but all that accomplished was to set it on fire.

"Yikes! Fire! " Dewey screamed, and threw the shirt into the river where it hissed and sank. Dewey's Jiffy Pop was still smoking like a wood furnace, so he grabbed a stick to lift the cremated popcorn bag out of the fire.

The three of us were rolling in laughter as Dewey opened the foil top. Black smoke erupted and the popcorn was a charcoal gray color.

"It looks slightly overdone," Chick said. That cracked us up again.

"It's fine," Dewey said. "I like it this way. It has a smoky taste."

He took a handful of the burnt popcorn and stuffed it into his mouth. He chewed a few times and spit the stuff into the fire.

"Whew, this is really smoky," he said.

Raucous laughter, again.

Dewey waded into the river to retrieve his shirt and hung it over a tent rope to dry.

"Anyone else for popcorn?" he asked.

"Make another one, Dewey, and I'll share it with you," Dougie said. This time Dewey held the Jiffy Pop away from the fire and it popped to perfection.

One by one, we began to yawn, and finally at two o'clock in the morning, we crawled into the tent and went to sleep.

Saturday was our last full day on the river. We had about twenty miles to travel to make it easy to reach our pick-up spot on Sunday with time to spare. We were to meet Dougie's dad at noon by the last bridge before the Mississippi. We thought four or five paddling miles on Sunday morning was about right. After breakfast, we paddled steady for several hours before stopping for lunch and a swim. We rested and then pushed on before stopping to set up camp again. Dougie and I were in one canoe and Dewey and Chick in the other and we got to a long stretch of river when Chick yelled, "We'll race you to the sandbar."

"You're on!" we said, accepting the challenge.

Paddling as fast as possible, we were neck and neck for a while and then they began to pull ahead of us. We had more weight in our canoe, and they got ahead of us and won the race. "Champions of the world!" Dewey made known, raising his paddle above his head. The two of them raised their paddles and bowed to the imaginary crowds.

Dougie and I just shook our heads. Two good friends, but so insane! Such a shame!

We journeyed on and came to an area that showed signs of a wind storm some time before. Trees were uprooted and the tops were moving back and forth in the river. "Watch us do a few fancy maneuvers around those trees," Chick said.

"You guys be careful. You'll get stuck," I warned. I may as well have spoken in Japanese for all the good it did because the two canoe champions were already amidst the fallen trees.

They were looking quite impressive when they misjudged a tree and the swiftness of the current and found themselves turned sideways against the current. It didn't take but a few seconds and they were swept into the branches and then pulled down so that water spilled into the canoe. Our canoe experts were soon in the water. The current swept the canoe upside down and it popped out on the other side of the tree. Dewey and Chick were also pulled under the tree and soon popped up downriver.

"Get over there!" Dougie directed, and we paddled toward them. Dewey and Chick had survived, so we chased down the runaway canoe. Then we attempted to rescue the gear they had lost. Thankfully we had taken the precaution to put most things in plastic bags, so we were able to recover it. We paddled to a sandbar and Chick and Dewey swam over to us.

"Watch us do trick canoe," I mocked. "Oh, dry up," Dewey blurted.

We laid the stuff that had taken a drink in the sun. Their sleeping bags were soaked and Dewey's clothes were missing.

"Didn't you put them in a bag?" I chided.

"I didn't think it mattered," Dewey said, glumly.

"Well, you didn't lose much; just underwear and T-shirts," Dougie teased.

"Yeah, I've still got the burned one," Dewey blurted.

This sandbar turned out to be another good one so we fished and made camp. We were becoming expert at this, and soon we were preparing our last supper on the river.

"Dewey, I think you should become a chef," Chick said.

"Yup, I agree. Dewey, you do good cooking," I complimented.

Dewey grinned, stirred the potatoes, and ripped one.

"Except for that, Dewey. I'd hate to have you doing that around my food all the time," Dougie said. We laughed.

We ate our last supper and then studied the starry sky as we reflected on the summer.

'Jeez! It was a great summer," Chick began. "No foolin'. I can't believe it's over," I sighed.

"Yeah, baseball, and going to the Braves game ... ," Dougie said.

"And our boat and raft," Dewey said.

"And poor Johnny and that Daredevil," Chick added. We shivered at the thought of that.

"That mean Mr. Mick at the pool. We sure fixed him," Dewey said, with a hearty laugh.

"And we took care of Roger and Mike at the scout campout," I recalled.

"And then you guys abandoned us in that cave. That still makes me mad," Dewey complained.

"How about the rotten-potato job? Those things smelled worse than Dewey," Dougie broke in.

Dewey raised his leg. "Careful, Douglas. I'm loaded and ready to shoot." We laughed until tears filled our eyes.

"And our friend, Faye. I'm so glad we got to know him," I said. We became quiet when we thought of him.

"We had a full summer," Dougie concluded.

"And now, school; the fun's over," Chick lamented.

"Well, it won't be too bad," I said. "We're gonna be eighth-graders, the big boys; top dog."

"Yeah, that's right. That won't be bad," Chick said. "But Dougie's in the other school," pouted Dewey.

"So what? That doesn't mean we can't do stuff after school and on weekends," Dougie said.

"Yeah. Hey, did you hear that Hunter Safety Class starts next week?" Chick said.

"Are you guys gonna take it?" someone asked.

It was unanimous. We all intended to show up for it.

"That will be fun-shooting guns and stuff," Dewey said. "When do you think the ice will be safe for fishing?" Chick wondered.

"We can get to the good spots on Gutweiler's on the ice," I said.

"I'm wondering if my dad will let me go deer hunting," Dougie said.

On and on we talked into the night. We didn't want to stop because that would signal the end, but we eventually got tired and crawled into the tent. Two sleeping bags were still wet, so we zipped open the two dry ones and we all crawled in, warm and snug, together; and my friends drifted off to sleep.

I listened to the night sounds, the crickets chirping, frogs kathunking, and an owl hooting far away in the distance. And, there were the sounds of Dewey, Dougie, and Chick sleeping. There was no better place in the whole world, or better friends than the ones I was with. These guys were the greatest! Together we were elephant boys, the west-side baseball team, fishing mates, and sleep-over buddies. We were like brothers, maybe, closer. We were the Musketeers: Athos, Porthos, Arimis and D'Artagnan; one fir all, all fir one.

I finally drifted off with visions of new adventures that awaited us just around the next bend in our young lives.

About the Author

Dan Bomkamp is an avid outdoor enthusiast. He grew up along the Wisconsin River and has made his home there since his college days at UW-LaCrosse. He has been involved in the sporting goods industry for many years and began his writing career by writing short stories for outdoor magazines in the early 1980s. He has hosted 30 foreign exchange students from 11 countries and has traveled to Europe to visit many of them.

His other books include: *The Adventures of Thunderfoot; More Adventures of Thunderfoot; Thanks Thunderfoot; Voyageur; Big Edna; Lost Flight; and Tag.* He lives in Muscoda, Wisconsin with his Boston Terrier, Buster, and his cat, Tigger. You can contact the author at *danbomkamp@live.com* or visit his website, *www.danbomkamp.com.*

www.ingramcontent.com/pod-product-compliance
Lightning Source LLC
Chambersburg PA
CBHW071158260626
47162CB00003B/1096